MW01247073

PEPPER

by

Raelyn Shaye

Gotham Books

30 N Gould St.
Ste. 20820, Sheridan, WY 82801
https://gothambooksinc.com/

Phone: 1 (307) 464-7800

Published by Gotham Books (May 27, 2023)

ISBN: 979-8-88775-261-7 (H)
ISBN: 979-8-88775-259-4 (P)
ISBN: 979-8-88775-260-0 (E)

CONTENTS

Introduction.. 1

Chapter 1 3

Chapter 2... 17

Chapter 3... 33

Chapter 4... 47

Chapter 5... 65

Chapter 6... 81

Chapter 7... 99

Chapter 8... 115

Chapter 9... 129

Chapter 10... 146

Chapter 11 163

Chapter 12... 180

Chapter 13... 197

Chapter 14... 214

Chapter 15..232

Chapter 16..249

Chapter 17..267

Chapter 18..285

Chapter 19..302

Chapter 20..319

This innovative, heart wrenching, fictional story is about a young girl by the name of Pepper, who went from living a typical city life to encountering a life of distress. It will keep you in suspense as you follow through some of the horrifying events that Pepper endures. The lifestyle that Pepper once knew, completely changes when she discovers her brother's "Memoir of Secrets" that exposes her fathers' connection to the death of their mother, including shocking truths about her father's past. Provided with evidence, Pepper continues to be in disbelief until the shocking truth finally unravels within her. As Pepper struggles to heal, she encounters new mysteries and heartbreaks that prevent her from finding a peaceful life. This suspenseful thriller takes you on a journey through the life of Pepper while keeping your curiosity alive.

Introduction

The mind can be erratic sometimes. A person can face such tremendous ordeals in life, that their conscious can be conceiving. What may seem real, may not in fact be a reality... Or is it?

Pepper is what they call me. In the beginning, I lived in the city with my father, Frank, and brother, Red. Our mother, Isabelle, had died of an unknown illness. She was one of the most loving women you could ever meet and knew how to keep us happy in our younger days. Isabelle could light up a room in seconds with her smiles. She caught the eyes of most men around town with her beauty.

Before she became ill, we were all elated. We always spent adequate time together. We were a contiguous family. Life appeared to be normal at the time.

So, I thought...

Everything started changing after the death of Isabelle. Red became angry at times and appeared very secretive about everything. My anticipation about what was going on in Red's head overpowered my mind to the point I started searching for answers in places I shouldn't have.

As answers started to arise, I encountered other overwhelming circumstances that I wasn't aware had went on. I became confused as I learned all the secrets my family had hidden. At the same time, I was just a child trying to figure out how to battle through life myself.

As I confronted all the obstacles life threw at me, I became more aware of my own self-conscious. Life as I once knew it, would never be the same again.

Chapter 1

It was a bright winter morning. Red and I walked through the thick snow to school. The roads were swamped with people everywhere, traveling to either school or work. The wind was so cold, we could see our breath. The elders nodded as we passed by. We stumbled to a sidewalk that had been shoveled off. Red and I decided to step on the clear path.

"Don't step on the crack, or you'll break your Nana's back" says Red.

"Oh, stop it!" I exclaimed. *"You are so superstitious, Red."*

Our grandma always made us call her Nana. She said the name "Grandma" made her feel old.

"Hey" Red said. *"Someday you will be old enough to understand. You can't go through your whole life thinking so innocent, Pepper. Bad things do happen to people, you know?"*

"No" I replied. *"I don't know."*

Red replied angrily, *"Well one day you will know!*

3

"Why are you being so mean?" I asked.

"Just forget about it," he replied shaking his head. *"You wouldn't understand if I told you anyway. Just go to class now."*

We had arrived at our school. It wasn't a long walk, just a few blocks away. It was one large school. I was in fifth grade, and Red was in ninth grade. I never saw him throughout the day, but he always waited on me after school to walk me home.

"Today we are starting with a scavenger hunt." Mrs. Josie said. *"I am going to put you in groups. Each group will have a different list of items to find around the classroom. After finding your items, you will explain ways the items can be used in everyday life."* She put us in groups and gave us the list of items to get started.

"What's on your list Pepper?" asked Candy.

"We are in the same group." I replied.

"Oh, right." said Candy.

Candy was a nice girl. She always tried her best to

make friends in the class, but for some reason no one really wanted to play with her. After a few minutes of hunting our items, we returned to our seats for group discussion.

"Can I sit by you?" Candy asked.

"Sure" I replied.

We finished our discussions, then moved on to music. This was my favorite part of the day. I enjoyed music because it infatuated me with all the different sounds the instruments made. Especially the piano, it was the most beautiful of all. I liked to settle in my spare time to practice playing where I resolved to teach myself. While listening to a song, I found similar sounds on the piano until I could play the whole song. It eventually became effortless for me.

At the end of the school day, I walked out to convene with Red. We always met at the same spot everyday. As we walked home, he avoided conversation.

"How was your day?" I asked.

He never replied. As he walked with his head down as if he was in deep meditation about something, I wandered what he could be thinking about.

Finally, Red spoke, *"You know, you are a lucky girl to have a brother like me."*

I glared at him with an erratic mind about what he had just said to me.

"What's that mean?" I replied.

"You will see someday Pepper." He said. *"You will figure it all out. But for now, it's my job to protect you, with mom not here anymore."*

I felt puzzled by some of the things Red spoke about. We arrived home and started our chores. I picked up around the house while Red washed dishes and other things. Frank usually worked late, so Red would cook for me. We ate noodles and chicken that night. Red wasn't an excellent cook, but we managed to survive. I remembered when Isabelle would cook Red and I tremendous meals all the time. We never went hungry with her around.

Afterwards, I went straight to my room and eased in bed thinking about Red. What could make him so hostile? Before, He was a nice brother to me. Ever since our mother died, he has changed. Was he upset about her death? My mind was like a straying ant, trying to find its way out of a hole. I had many questions that I couldn't figure out answers to and I feared asking Red.

I awakened the next morning to Red yelling, *"Come on Pepper, get up! We are going to be late for school!"*

I jumped up out of bed quickly to get dressed. We didn't have time for breakfast so we went straight to school. Red wouldn't talk to me on our walk to school that morning. After arriving to school, we separated to our classes.

With everything on my mind, I had a hard time paying attention to the teacher. All I could give thought to was my brother. He had me worried from the night before.

"May I go to the nurse office Mrs. Josie?" I asked.

"Do you not feel well today, Pepper?" She asked.

"No, no not really." I replied.

"Alright, go see the nurse then." Mrs. Josie said.

As I walked calmly down the long hallway to the nurse's office, I couldn't help but consider leaving school. At that moment, I ran into Candy.

7

"Why are you not in class?" asked Candy.

I looked at her for what seemed to be a long time.

She repeated," Why *are you not in class?"*

I grabbed her by the hand and told her to follow me.

"Where are we going Pepper?" She asked once we got outside.

"To the graveyard." I replied." *I just need to go see my mommy. I haven't been to visit her since she-- since she died. Just come on."*

"Won't we get in trouble for leaving school?" She asked.

"Look! You can go back to school if you want but I am going to visit my mommy's grave!" I replied angrily.

For a moment, I reminded myself of Red, how he always yelled in response to things. Now here I am doing the same with Candy. Her face looked as if she was in shock, but she decided to go with me.

We strutted down the street to the graveyard. Candy

followed closely behind me. After getting there, I debated if I had made the right choice to go. The graveyard looked dreadful and intimidating. I gripped hands with Candy as we ambled through the front gates of the graveyard. Wow! I thought. The grave yard wasn't how I recalled it being months before. Maybe it just looked alarming because no one else was there. We walked toward the area I thought Isabelle was buried.

As we passed headstones, we read the names aloud.

"Mary... Robert... Daniel... Mathew... Sally... Ben..."

I got an eccentric feeling within me the further we strolled. I began to run with Candy following meticulously behind me.

All of a sudden, I plunged over a rock and fell to the ground. When I looked up, I seen a headstone that read, ***"In Beloved Memory of Cherry."*** We had stumbled across a grave of a little girl. I sat anxiously gawking at her grave for a few minutes or so.

"I wander how she died." Candy said.

"I don't know." I replied. *"Maybe we can find out*

somehow. Looks like she's been dead for few years. It says she was only eight years old when she died. Let's go."

As I started to gradually walk away, something caught my eye. It was sparkling in the sunlight. I reached down to grasp it with my hand. It was a small necklace that had a charm in the shape of a heart hanging on it. I figured someone dropped it, so I put it in my pocket, and meandered on to find my mom's grave. We finally came to Isabelle's grave site. I sat in silence staring at her headstone.

"Well, aren't you going to talk to her?" asked Candy.

"Talk to her?" I replied. *"Dead people can't hear you. You don't talk to them; you just visit with them. Sit and be quiet for awhile Candy."*

We sat awhile longer in the absence of sound. Eventually, I began rambling about my life, how happy we were, then mom dying, and how Red was irritated now. I conscientiously couldn't hold it all in anymore. It was like my mind was ready to explode. Candy sat in lull listening as I revealed my life.

"Do you want me to ask your brother what is wrong?"

asked Candy.

"No!" I replied. *"And you can't tell anyone about what I told you today. You hear?"*

"Yes." She replied quietly.

We raced back to our school with neither one of us speaking to each other. As we approached the school, Red proceeded toward me.

"Where have you been Pepper?" He asked in a demanding voice. *"Don't you know everyone has been looking for you? Why would you just run off like that?"*

Red kept demanding answers out of me, but I stood with my head descended in silence. I became apprehensive to speak and wanted to be left alone. He marched me home, then instructed me to go in my room until dinner was ready. Resting on my bed, I peered around captivated in thought.

Red came to get me when dinner was ready. Casually eating, there was still an air of tension between us.

"Red." I said.

He never looked at me, so I continued talking.

"How do you find out how a person died? I am just asking so don't get mad at me Red."

He took a deep breath and then replied, *"I don't know, the library, I guess. Why are you so worried about that now? You shouldn't be worried about them kinds of things. Go collect rocks or something. And where were you today? Answer me that."*

"I was at the graveyard." I replied quietly under my breath.

Red glanced at me in a rapacious way. Then he hobbled out of the kitchen as he told me to go to bed.

I woke up the next morning shivering under my blanket. It felt like the temperatures were dropping outside. I looked at the clock on the wall only to notice it was past time to go to school. I aroused from my bed to listen, but it was quiet. So, I climbed out of bed and went to the kitchen, but no one was home. In my mind, I concluded it was peculiar that I would be left home alone.

As I returned to my room, I tried to envision how far the library was from our house. The anticipation of how

Cherry died still wandered my mind, so I dressed warm to go on a journey to find the library. As I roamed the streets, a man approached me. He asked why I wasn't in school. I informed him I was traveling to the library.

"Library?" the man asked.

"Yes." I replied. *"You see, I went to the graveyard yesterday and stumbled over a grave of a little girl, named Cherry. I want to know how she died. She was only eight years old; you know. I thought only old people died?"*

"I know who you are talking about." the man replied sadly.

"You do?" I asked. *"Well, what happened to her? Do you know what happened to her?"*

"Yes, I-- I am afraid I do know what happened to her." He said as he sat on a bench.

"Well, what?" I asked with curiosity.

He began to slowly tell me the story of the little girl, *"Well you see, my name is Paul. That was my niece. Her father, my brother, killed her."*

13

I sat quietly watching Paul trying to speak, as he held back his tears.

"My brother claimed she was too difficult to handle. She had an incurable disease, and my brother didn't know how to take care of her." Paul became silent.

He started speaking again. *"She was a good little girl, I thought. Her father drank all the time, and would beat on her. By the time anyone found out, it was too late to save her."*

"Where was her mom?" I asked.

Paul replied, *"Her mother left when she was a baby. Her mother came from a strict background, and her parents made her give the baby up. So, my brother raised her. No one has heard from her mother in years. I don't even think she knows her daughter is dead."*

Paul looked dismayed so I didn't ask him anything else. We sat on the bench together observing the cars go by. After awhile, I told him I had to go home.

As I shuffled down the street, I speculated about the tragic story of Cherry. It was morbid to think how a father could do something so horrible to his child. How could no one know? I contemplated to myself the whole way home. Others said *"hello"* as they passed, but I just nodded and continued walking.

After returning home, I waited in my room for Red. Soon, he entered through the door.

"Are you hungry?" He asked.

"A little." I replied.

"Let's go." He said with a stern voice.

I followed him down the street to a small diner. We shuffled in to find a seat.

"Where did you get money?" I asked.

"Look, don't worry about it Pepper. Just order something." said Red.

We ordered food and began eating.

"Why didn't you wake me up for school today?" I asked.

"Figured you could use a day off after what you pulled yesterday." He replied. *"You know, you really shouldn't be*

wondering out there by yourself in such a big city. You could get lost one day or taken."

I glanced downward as I ate, not daring to say a word about today's adventure.

We went for a walk after eating and arrived home right before Frank walked in.

He asked what we were up to.

"We were just getting ready to go to bed." replied Red before I could say anything.

For some reason, I sensed Red didn't want our dad to know we were out. I found it odd, but I departed to bed without questioning anything.

Chapter 2

It seemed like a long night with difficulty sleeping. The sounds of the wind were intense. A snow storm was blowing in. I cuddled in my bed gazing out the window until nodding away, but I wasn't asleep long before woken up by Red again for school. Without being hungry, I skipped out the door to school.

On our way, Red initiated conversation with me.

"I don't want you leaving the school for any reason today." He said. *"You hear me, Pepper? You're lucky I begged them to not call dad the other day. If he finds out you are running around like that by yourself, we will both be in trouble. Are you listening to me?"*

"Yes, I understand," I replied. *"I won't leave the school today, Red. I promise. You don't have to worry about me. I won't do nothing like that again."*

"Good," He replied. *"It's good you finally got your mind straightened out. You need to worry about kid stuff, and leave the adult stuff alone for now."*

We arrived at school and proceeded to our classes. It was the same routine every school morning.

"Good morning, Pepper, we missed you yesterday," said Mrs. Josie.

I smiled as I stepped into the classroom.

"Pepper, where were you yesterday?" asked Candy.

"I found out about that little girl, you know, the one from the graveyard," I replied. *"I found out how she died. Her father killed her. He got drunk one night and just killed her. I talked to her uncle, and he said the abuse had been going on for awhile. But it was too late by the time anyone found out about it."*

"You-- you actually talked to her uncle?" She asked.

"Well, yes, I did. His name is Paul." I replied. *"I was on my way to the library when he stopped me and asked why I wasn't in school. I told him why and then he told me he was her uncle. He is still sad about her death."*

"Everyone takes their seats," said Mrs., Josie.

"You better not tell anyone," I said to Candy as we

18

were sitting down. *"My brother finds out; I will get in trouble. So just keep quiet."*

The school day flew by fast. I didn't feel like doing much, so I remained to myself most of the day. When school ended, I fled to the meeting spot. Like everyday, Red escorted me toward home. After we returned home, we ate, then went to bed. The exhaustion of the day's adventure, put me straight to sleep. A few hours later, I was awakened by the sounds of two people arguing. I couldn't hear what the argument was about, but I recognized the voices of Red and Frank.

"What could they be arguing about this late at night?"

I thought to myself. I crawled over to the door to see if I could hear anything. Mom was mentioned, but I couldn't quite make out what was being said. Finally, after about an hour of arguing, it became silent. I had assumed they both decided to go to bed, so I went back to sleep as well.

The next day, I slept most of the morning. It was a weekend, so there was no school to attend. I inched into the kitchen where I found my brother, Red, cooking breakfast. I sat at the kitchen table waiting on Red to give me my food. He served me breakfast, then sat down to eat also.

"What were you and papa arguing about last night?" I asked.

"You heard our conversation, Pepper?" Red replied.

"Well, yes-- I mean no! I heard arguing, but I couldn't hear what was being said." I said in a scared voice.

"You listen here little girl! You just stop snooping around in others business!" Red angrily said.

"But I wasn't snooping Red. You were arguing loud enough for me to hear it." I replied.

"Just leave it alone Pepper! I am going to take care of this." Red explained.

"Take care of what?" I asked.

"Mind your own business, Pepper. Let it go and don't talk about it anymore! I am going out for awhile, and you just stay here and be good." He replied.

Red slammed his plate in the sink, and flew out of the kitchen angrily.

I remained at the table after Red left the kitchen.

Suddenly, I wasn't hungry anymore.

"Why was everything a big deal to Red?" I thought.

At that moment, I became determined to find something out. I was tired of wandering all the time and needed to know what was wrong with my brother.

Red left the house a short time later. Then, I trampled into his room after he left. He would be very hostile if he caught me snooping through his things. Red was a reserved person who didn't like to talk much about himself. I knew I had to hurry and find something before he returned back home. Confused as to what I was looking for, I started scrambling through everything. After searching in his drawers, closet, under the bed, and behind his door, I couldn't find anything out of place that would give me a clue as to what was wrong with him. I sat on his bed discouraged for a minute.

"Wait, what is this?" I thought.

As I sat down on my brother's bed, I could feel something under me. I reached under his blanket and grasped a small book. It wasn't a regular book and without title.

21

"Hmm". I thought to myself. *"What could it be?"*

I opened the book slowly. It was Red's handwriting inside the book.

"Did my brother write a book?" I thought excitedly.

At that moment, I heard someone entering the front door, so I put the book back and scurried out of his room quickly. It was Red.

*"What are you up to Pepper?" H*e asked as I quietly walked into the living room.

"Nothing," I replied. *"Just hanging around the house trying to find something to do."*

Red stared at me strangely as he grabbed what he needed.

"Well, just go play in your room for awhile. And stay out of trouble," he said as he walked back out the door.

I relaxed on the couch for a few minutes trying to determine why Red would want to hide his book. I deliberated as to whether or not he planned on showing everyone the book after he had finished writing it. Maybe I shouldn't read it. I pertained to thought for a minute. I knew I wanted to read this book. The anticipation to find out what Red wrote was overwhelming. My anxious self had to at least check it out.

After waiting a few more minutes to make sure he was gone, I went back to his room to get the book out again. I held it in my hands as I glared at it. In a way I felt guilty, like I was invading my brother's privacy, but I was distressed from all the secrets. To ease my own mind, I had desired to read it. This chaos from Red was starting to annoy me. Red wouldn't find out anyway. I would read it and not say anything.

The thought of Red finding me in his room had me shaken. I had to be careful not to get caught because I wouldn't know what to say if he seen me reading the book he wrote. His anger at me would be extreme. Quickly, I tried to read his book.

"My Secrets," It read.

"Today was a good day. Mom took us to the store and let us pick out what we wanted. Pepper picked out a toy, but not me. No, I am growing up. So, I picked out a deck of cards. My parents don't know it, but I meet with my friends once or twice a month after school to play cards for money. I won a little. I keep it stashed in a secret place where no one will find it. One day when I need it, I will go get it out of hiding.

Until next time...."

"My Secrets,"

"Mom made the best homemade biscuits and gravy for breakfast. Dad didn't join us as usual. It almost feels like our family is starting to fall apart. Dad gets really jealous over mom. I think it is because she gets so much attention from others. After breakfast we went out for awhile. Mom likes being outdoors, we are always doing something together. We went for a walk. We had a lot of fun today, just like we always do. Wish Dad would of went.

Until next time...."

"My Secrets,"

"To my surprise, Dad has been coming around again. It's a little strange though. He insists on helping Mom with the cooking and stuff. We have never seen Dad want to cook much. But I think Mom is just happy that Dad is wanting to be a family again. Everything seems to be getting back to normal. Dad has even started making Mom breakfast in bed. She smiles every time. Today we went swimming. We splashed and played half the day. Pepper really enjoyed it. After a couple hours of being there, Mom said she wasn't feeling well. Dad bought her a drink, but that made her feel worse. So, we left and went home so Mom could lay down awhile. Until next time...."

"My Secrets,"

"Today was a good day, but Dad is acting more strange than ever before. He has been spending most of his spare time in the basement. He told me and Pepper that we weren't allowed to go down there and play anymore. That he turned it into his workshop now. I've been really curious what kind of work he actually does in the basement. I want to sneak down there, but he keeps it locked up. Another thing I have been curious about is why we have never met his family and only mom's. I finally

asked him about it. He told me he didn't have a family. I asked
Mom about it and she said my dad's family was in a bad car
accident and were killed. I thought this to be strange. Everyone
was killed? Or maybe he lied.

Until next time..."

I skimmed through a few random pages just to get an idea of things Red wrote about. He talked abundantly about things we did daily. As I continued reading, memories of Isabelle came back to me. I had wished our mother were still alive because I missed her extremely bad. The memories took me back to the days where we were all in high spirits as we did family things together. Red spoke a lot of our mother in his book and how much he adored her. I flipped to the middle of the book to see what else Red had to say. I eventually came to entries that had been written about the times when Isabelle was severely ill. These were hard times for Red and I.

"My Secrets,"

"Mom is ill again. This has become an everyday thing now.
We try to spend time together, and go out to do things, but Mom
always becomes sick. The doctors can't figure it out. They ran
tests, but can't find what is wrong with her. Some days are

worse than others. If only we could figure it out, we could help her feel better. My Dad is acting strange still. He is cooking full time now. He just shows no emotion. Dad doesn't seem upset at all. wander why? I am so confused about everything that is going on around me. Until next time...."

You know, come to think about it, I never remembered Frank being upset about Isabelle. It had me wandering why now too. As I pondered on what Red had wrote, I heard him return home. I threw the book under Red's pillow before scurrying out of his room. I met him at the door as he came inside. It had become obvious that I was up to something by the way I reacted. I stood nervously by the front door waiting on Red to notice that I was in his room.

"How was your day?" I asked.

"It was good," He replied.

Red paused for a moment. I became increasingly horrified of what he was contemplating. He glared at me with a malevolent look in his eyes. I knew he was thinking about me being in his room.

"What am I going to tell him?" I thought to myself. *"I*

didn't know what to say! Think Pepper, think!"

Red opened his mouth to speak. It was like watching a movie in slow motion. He had been acting so strangely, I didn't know what to expect next out of him.

"Why are you acting so nervous, Pepper?" He finally asked. *"What did you do while I was gone?"*

"Nothing. I uhh--" I was stumbling over words to say. *"I watched some T.V. and umm-- "*

"Yeah, yeah, whatever Pepper. I don't even think I want to know. Just stay out of trouble." Red interrupted.

Red strolled down the hallway to his room. This was the moment of truth. I would have to admit I was in his room. He turned around to see me slowly creeping up behind him. I wanted to make sure he wasn't going to find out.

"Why are you following me?" Red asked in a curious voice.

"Me? Oh, I am not following you. I was just--- going to the bathroom. Yeah, that's what I was doing." I replied.

Red stared at me silently as I went into the bathroom

and shut the door. I pushed my ear up against the door to see if I could hear anything. I listened as the sounds of Red's boots hit the floor one step at a time.

"Boom... boom... boom... boom..."

My heart was beating excessively, as I concentrated on his every move. Sweat started to drip down my face. The temperature in the room suddenly felt like it had increased to a hundred degrees.

"Please... please don't let him find out about me reading his book." I thought to myself desperately.

Suddenly I heard the footsteps again. *"Boom...boom...boom...boom..."* Then there was a soft knock on the bathroom door.

"Pepper, are you okay in there?" asked this stern voice on the other side of the bathroom door.

"Yes." I replied. *"I will be out in a minute."*

After a few minutes of collecting my thoughts together, I opened the bathroom door gently. I thought for sure Red would be standing there waiting on me as the door opened, but he wasn't. As I observed both ways down the hallway to make sure no one was there, I ran into my room as fast as I could. I glared out the window watching the snow fall until Red entered to check on me. We stood gazing into each other's eyes, wandering which one of us was going to speak first.

Then he spoke softly to me. *"Pepper, I want you to get some sleep tonight. We are going to go on a long journey tomorrow."*

"Where are we going?" I asked.

Red replied, *"Do you always have to ask questions about everything? Why can't you just do what your told without asking questions? That gets annoying you know. Just pack a few clothes, and wait for me to say when we are leaving. And don't breathe a word of this to anyone. You don't need to go stirring up any trouble right now.*

"Okay," I said as I sat down on my bed.

I sat a few more minutes, after Red left the room, before packing some clothes.

"Where was Red taking me?" I thought. *"What about*

school? What was he hiding? Does it have anything to do with what he wrote in the book? Why won't he just tell me anything?"

Being confused, I had many questions continuously flowing through my head at that moment. I knew I had to read more of that book, but I was frightened. I wasn't sure if I wanted to chance being caught by Red.

"If I could read more of Red's secrets, it would probably answer some of my questions." I thought.

It weighed heavily on my mind while packing a few clothes and wasn't going to give up. I was determined to find answers. If Red wasn't going to tell me anything, I would find out myself. I finished packing, then went to the kitchen for dinner settling at the table to eat with Red.

"Pepper, I have to go out for awhile tonight, to-- to get things arranged." said Red. *"Don't worry about nothing. I will take care of everything."*

Even though I had no knowledge of what he was conversing about, I didn't ask any questions. I understood he would become angry with me again. So, I continued eating.

"What, no questions this time from my curious sister?" Red asked sarcastically.

I never replied. Sometimes I theorized whether Red liked scheming to get me wandering. We finished eating dinner, then went to get ready for bed. Regards to where Red could be going, at this time of night, engrossed my mind. I decided to pretend I was asleep until Red was ready to leave because I wanted to sneak back into his room. Curiosity was on my mind about what else was in his secret book. I couldn't stop thinking about it.

Everything Red had written about Isabelle kept my interest. The memories of her overwhelmed my mind. I enjoyed thinking about her. Isabelle was an inspiration to me. As I lay still in the dark, I heard my door squeak open.

"Pepper." Red whispers. *"Are you awake?"*

I clammed up in my bed as I held my eyes tightly shut. After a few seconds, my door quietly shuts, but I didn't move until I could hear Red leaving the house.

Chapter 3

It was mortally dark in my room. I couldn't see a thing, so I let the memories of Isabelle dwell upon my mind.

We took a vacation to the mountains once. Isabelle liked to hike and explore. We camped while we were there. I remember the trip being a lot of fun.

"Are we almost there yet?" Red asked.

"Almost!" said Isabelle excitedly. *"You two are going to have an amazing time, when we get there!"*

Any time with Isabelle was amazing to me. She always had a way of taking a boring situation, and turning it into a fun event.

"Here we are!" She exclaimed after a few minutes.

We drove up to the campground we were going to be staying at. It was packed with people. Frank went in to pay for everything while the rest of us waited in the car. I glanced outside the windows of the car. I could see a big beach with brownish color sand and big water slides with a pool. The campground accommodated more swimming areas than I had ever seen. Everyone on the beach and pool area appeared to be enjoying themselves.

"When do we get to go swimming?" asked Red

"Soon son. We have to get our camping stuff set up, and then we can go have fun. Just be patient." replied Isabelle.

Red squirmed around in his seat like a worm. When he got excited, he couldn't sit still. Finally, Frank returned to the car and drove around the campground until we came to the spot we were staying at. Red abruptly jumped out of the car.

"Calm down son." Frank said. *"No need to rush. We have all day to swim. That water isn't going anywhere."*

The rest of us piled out of the car slowly. We all helped unload the car and get things set up at the camp site. After we were finished, we hiked to the beach. On the way, a trolley stopped beside us. So, we hopped on the trolley and it took us to the beach area. Red was so excited that he tripped as he got off the trolley. Frank demanded him to slow down and be more careful. I was astonished by all the people around me. There were other children playing on the beach building sand castles. Red and Frank went on to the water slides and pool area, while Isabelle and I went to the beach. I sat on the sand with my mom watching the small waves come in to the shore.

"It's beautiful out here. Look at that water. Maybe we can ask daddy to take us boating later." Isabelle said.

"Yes, maybe." I replied. *"Can I bury you in the sand mommy?"*

"Of course." She responded with a smile.

I scooped sand into my hands, then poured it all over Isabelle. She looked silly lying with sand all over her. I couldn't help but chuckle while I was burying her.

"So, you think it's funny to bury your mom?" She said as she chuckled herself.

All of a sudden, she flew up out of the sand like a tornado swirling through town.

"Roar!" Isabelle yelled loudly.

Sand went flying everywhere, all over me. It startled me when she came up so quickly. I jumped backward a little.

"Did I scare you, my princess?" Isabelle asked.

"Yes." I said while laughing.

"Let's go get wet and wash off this sand." She said.

We jumped in the water and swam for awhile. Then Frank and Red came over so we could go eat. We hiked back to our camp site to start a fire. For the remainder of the evening, we rested around the fire cooking hot dogs. Right before dark, we roasted marshmallows. It was a good family night together telling spooky stories until bed time.

The next morning, we piled out early to hike in the mountains. We went out for breakfast at a small diner. After we finished eating, we continued to our destination. The mountain was extremely big to me. We put on our gear, and started our walk. As we hiked up the mountain trail, we explored the beautiful nature around us. We observed many trees and bugs as we traveled. Frank and Red picked up different bugs along the way to examine them. Red tried to scare me with the spiders because he knew I didn't like them.

"Look Pepper! A spider!" said Red.

"Ewww! Gross! Get it away from me Red!" I cried out.

"You two stop." Isabelle said.

About half way up the mountain, we stopped to take a break. As I relaxed on a big rock to catch my breath, a hissing sound grabbed my attention. I leaned over the big rock I was sitting on to glance around and observed movement coming from the leaves on the ground beside me. All of a sudden, a snake slowly lifted its head out of the leaves.

"Ahhh!" I squealed as I lunged off the rock briskly.

"What! What is wrong?" Isabelle asked frantically.

"There's a snake over there behind that big rock!" I replied scared.

I curled up like a little baby in my mother's lap while my father grabbed the snake.

It was terrifying, so I kept my distance. Frank paraded toward me holding the snake.

"This snake is harmless." he said as he threw the snake back into the woods. *"Let's get moving again."*

We finally made it to the top of the mountain. The views were fascinating. A few clouds covered the sky as the sun brilliantly shined through them. I positioned myself next to Isabelle observing the steep fall below us.

"Stay away from the ledge my dear. We wouldn't want you to fall." She responded in a whispering voice.

We admired the views awhile longer before heading back. After arriving at the campground, we spent time together swimming again and eating dinner. We explored different site adventures the next few days before ending our vacation and returning home.

More memories that stayed with me were family reunions we attended. The last reunion we visited was right before Isabelle died.

"Mom, are you sure you are feeling up to going this year?" Red asked.

"Yes. I always go. I will be fine. Besides, we only get together like this once a year. I never miss a chance to be with my family." Isabelle replied.

It was always reunions on Isabelle's side of the family. We never met Frank's family, but it never bothered me back then. There were many different foods set up as a big buffet, and games that all of the kids played. Isabelle usually helped with everything. The last year she was alive, she couldn't do anything but sit on the sidelines.

This was the weakest I had ever seen Isabelle. She had always been one of the strongest people I'd known, and now she was one of the weakest. So much changed in a year's time. It was almost like she was almost helpless now, just waiting to die. I believe she knew it was coming. I'd never seen her cry about it though. She considered it to be a part of life. I had a conversation with her one time about it.

"Mommy, are you going to die?" I asked.

"Everyone dies sometimes sweetie." She replied.

"Why?" I asked curiously.

"It's just a part of life, Pepper." She replied.

Isabelle didn't like conversing much about things that were negative. She kept a positive attitude in life, even when something was bad.

There were many times Isabelle took us for picnics. She would pack sandwiches in her big basket, and we would all go to the park for lunch. It was a big park that had paths for walking, several different play areas, and a big field to run around. After we ate, I went to play on the playground for awhile before we left.

Other memories were visits with my grandparents. They were always fun. Their town had a small quick stop store a few short blocks from where they lived. When we visited our grandparents, they gave Red and I a whole dollar to share. I thought it to be a lot of money, but Red always wanted more. We traveled on foot to the store so we could spend every penny we had on candy. The store had a variety of candies to choose from. We trotted back home like happy little bees getting nectar from a flower in the summer. Our grandparents loved spoiling Red and I. They put smiles on our faces every time we came around.

I recalled a canoe trip we went on. We were only allowed to have two people per boat. Isabelle and Red were in one, and Frank and I were in another. I wanted to ride with Isabelle, but Frank said Red could help her paddle better than I. Isabelle made me wear a life jacket while on the river. It was bulky and tight so I didn't like it. I complained to Isabelle about wearing the jacket.

"Mom, why do I have to wear this?" I asked.

"It will keep you safe Pepper. If you fall into the water, you will sink to the bottom and drown. But if you have a life jacket on, it will keep you floating above the water." Isabelle replied.

"Well, it's tight on me. I don't like it." I said in a complaining voice.

"It's supposed to be tight. That way if you fall out of the canoe it doesn't slip off of you." She replied back firmly.

"Okay." I sighed sadly.

We jumped into our boats and paddled down the river. The sights were beautiful. The canoe rocked a little, so it scared me. Frank assured me that it wouldn't turn over. We approached a mid-stopping point where we could get out of our canoes. I plopped down on the side of the river bank next to Isabelle while Frank and Red explored in the woods.

"Mom. Can I ride with you the rest of the way?" I asked.

"No sweetie. I need Red to help me paddle my canoe."

Isabelle sweetly replied.

"But I could do it for you mommy." I said desperately.

"Pepper, you are going to ride with your father." Isabelle replied. *"I will let you ride with me another time. Let's go find your brother and father so we can get back on the--"*

"BOO!" Red jumped out of the trees yelling.

Frank came out laughing, *"Ha ha.. Did you two get frightened?"*

"Good one." Isabelle said. *"We better get back on the river before it starts getting dark."*

We finished our canoeing, then proceeded to eat before going home. Isabelle tucked me tightly into bed and read me a bed time story. I didn't remember much of it because I dozed off to sleep soon after she began reading. I admired when Isabelle sat in my room reading until I fell asleep. It made me feel content.

More memories flowed in my thoughts as I continued to lay in the dark. Fishing trips were something Frank arranged for the family. Frank loved to fish, so Isabelle would gather food for us to stay most of the day. We always ended up at a big lake. There were hardly no trees for shade. Isabelle forced Red and I wear sunblock. The lake was about an hour drive from our house. I hated the drive, but had fun once we arrived at our destination.

We loaded everything into the car to commute to the lake. After the long drive, we unloaded the car.

"Red, come over here and help your father." said Isabelle.

"Why can't Pepper help him?" Red asked.

"Red!" Isabelle loudly spoke.

"Yes ma'am. Be there in a minute." Red replied in a soft voice.

Isabelle never had a temper, but she would show you who the boss was if it was required. Red helped Frank get the fishing poles set up as I glanced over at my pole.

"Pepper, you are going to learn how to bait your own hook today." Frank said.

"But the hooks are sharp daddy. I have never been allowed to touch them." I replied.

"Today, you will be allowed to touch it. You just have to be careful so it doesn't poke you." Frank firmly spoke. *"Go over there and get one of them worms out of that small white container laying over by your mom."*

Slowly walking over to where Isabelle was sitting, I reached down to pick up the white container full of worms. I opened the lid, and grabbed a worm. It felt slimy and gross. It wiggled between my fingers trying to get away. I held it tightly so I wouldn't drop it.

"Pepper! Come on now. Your daddy ain't got all day to fool around. We are going to miss the fish biting." Frank yelled.

"I'm coming daddy. This worm is wiggling too much. I can't hardly hold on to it." I replied.

I ran over to Frank. He was getting really impatient waiting on me. I got down on my knees beside him holding the worm. Frank was holding the hook in one of his hands.

"Now you slowly take the hook and slide it through the

44

worm, like this. " Frank explained, as he grabbed my hand and showed me how to put the worm onto the hook. *"There you go. Now you are ready to cast your pole out into the water and catch some fish, Pepper. "* Frank said as he handed me my pole back.

"But my hands are slimy dad. " I whined.

"Stop crying and go wipe your hands in the grass. Better yet, just go wash them off in the lake. It won't hurt you none. " Frank replied.

After bending over to clean my hands in the lake, I cast my pole out to see if I could catch a fish. I never caught anything before. Red has caught a few miniature fish, but Frank was the only lucky one to catch big fishes. They never kept any of the fish. The fish would be thrown back into the lake. What was the point of going fishing if we couldn't keep them?

We settled around the food Isabelle brought, eating while waiting on the fish to bite. As soon as it started getting dark, we packed up to go home. Fishing wasn't my favorite thing to do, but I enjoyed going on different trips with my family.

After returning home, it was the same routine after any other trip we had taken. We unloaded the car and Isabelle tucked me tightly into bed. I really missed them days with Isabelle. If only she had not gotten sick, she would still be here to tuck me tightly into bed every night. I continued to visualize the times with Isabelle for awhile longer as I lay in my dark room.

Many other trips we took were on my mind also. Even though we never lived fancy, we were always traveling somewhere. One thing I will never forget Isabelle saying to me; *"It's better to have little and live your life freely, than to live in royalty and have your freedom taken."*

Chapter 4

After Frank went to sleep, Red finally left. That was my signal to sneak back into Red's room to read his book. As I ambled quietly down the hallway to Red's room, a door slams open behind me.

"What are you doing out of bed?" yelled Frank.

I stopped and gasped in fear.

"Well, answer me young lady!" Frank yelled.

I could barely talk. *"I-- uhh... I am going to Red's room Daddy."* I replied in a quiet voice.

Frank stomped over to Red's door and jerked it open. He stood in the doorway for a minute looking around the room.

"And where is your brother Pepper?" Frank asked.

At that moment, I started spilling the beans. *"I don't know. I was supposed to pack some clothes for a trip and he is out taking care of some things and-- and...*

"Wait." Frank interrupted. *"A trip for what? And what is he taking care of?"*

"I don't know." I replied. *"He has been acting really strange since mamma died and he won't tell me anything. He says he needs to protect me. He told me to pack some clothes and he was taking me somewhere."*

"Hmm." Frank responded. *"Pepper, go back to bed. I will take care of this in the morning."*

As I leaped back into my room, I didn't dare ask Frank what was going on. Frank would probably make things better with Red. Maybe Red would start acting normal now. I tried to stay awake until my brother returned from doing his business, but I fell asleep.

The next morning, I was awakened by men talking. I glanced out of my room and saw Frank being questioned by police officers. One of the officers approached me.

"Good morning, Pepper." an officer said. *"May I ask you a few questions about your brother, Red?"*

Frank spoke up angrily. *"You can't question her about anything! She is just a child. She doesn't know anything. She was in bed all night."*

"Take him to the station for further questioning." said one officer to another.

I watched as they drug my father out of the room in handcuffs.

"Why are you taking my father to jail?" I asked.

"We are not taking your father to jail. Just to the station so we can figure some things out." replied the officer. *"Can I ask you some questions?"*

"Yes." I replied.

"When was the last time you seen Red?" The Officer asked.

"Well, last night, at dinner." I hesitantly replied.

"Did he say anything unusual?" He asked.

"Unusual?" I asked confused.

"Yes, strange, not right." replied the officer.

"Well, he's been acting strange lately." I said with a

confused look.

"How so?" The officer asked.

"Just ever since mommy died, he has been acting different." I replied. *"He has been hiding things from me. He won't tell me nothing. So, I went looking through his room to find my own answers. I found a book he wrote and..."*

"A book." the officer interrupted. *"What book are you talking about Pepper?"*

"This book, hold on I will get it." I replied.

I went to Red's room to get the book. The officer followed behind me. When I reached for the book, it was gone.

"But it was right here." I explained. *"There was a book that my brother wrote right here!"*

"Did you read this book?" the officer asked.

"Some of it." I said. *"I was on my way back in there last night after my brother left to read more of it, but that's when my father caught me sneaking down the hallway. He got angry with me and made tell him what was going on."*

"What did you tell your father?" asked the officer.

"I told him that Red asked me to pack some clothes, that he was taking me on a trip to protect me, and how Red was out taking care of some things before our trip." I replied.

"How did your father respond to what you told him?" The officer asked.

"He told me to go to bed that he would take care of everything." I replied.

"What do you think your brother was trying to protect u from?" asked the officer.

"I don't know. He wouldn't say." I said quietly.

"Pepper, can you tell me what you read in the book?" The officer asked.

"It was mostly about what Red did, and about mommy. He talked about mommy being sick and stuff. I was going to read more before I was caught by Daddy. I was just trying to find out why Red was acting so strange all the time. What he was being so secretive about. I didn't mean to cause any trouble." I replied.

"What makes you think you caused any trouble?" asked the officer.

"Well, you are here, and Daddy is angry. So, I must have caused some trouble." I replied.

"Do you know why I am here, Pepper?" The officer asked.

"NO. I guess not." I replied.

"Your father called, and said that Red is missing. That he never came home last night. So, we are trying to figure out where your brother could have gone. Do you know anything about your brother's where abouts?" The officer asked.

"No. and he wouldn't have left without me anyway. I know he will be back to get me today because he said he would. Just wait, you will see." I replied with confidence.

We waited for what seemed to be hours. I settled at the kitchen table while several police officers searched through our house. I wandered what they were looking for. One of the officers finally walked over to me holding Red's book in his hand.

"Where did you find it?" I asked.

"Is this the book you were referring to?" the officer asked.

"Yes!" I said with joy. *"Where was it?"*

"We found it in a packed bag of clothes." the officer replied. *"Your brother must have put it in there when he was packing his clothes." "of course!"* I replied. *"He wouldn't have left his book, so he packed it. My brother is very smart you know."*

The officers hovered over each other while glancing through Red's book.

"Can I read the book too?" I asked one of the officers as I was tugging on his pant leg.

"No. you go sit over there and let us read it to see if we can figure out anything. We will talk to you in a minute Pepper." the officer said firmly.

As I sat with an angry face, I didn't know why everyone kept me in suspense all the time. I determined my life would stay full of unanswered questions.

It had been way past a minute and the officers were still reading through Red's book. He would be so mad if he stumbled through the front door to see that others had his book. I waited impatiently in hopes that Red would return quickly and catch them in the act.

After another hour had passed, there was still no sign of Red. I was getting really tired of waiting. Then, one of the officers picked his phone up to make a call. I was curious who he could be calling. After a couple minutes, he approached me. The officer told me I would have to go to a facility to stay while they tried to find my brother.

"But what about daddy?" I asked.

"Your dad will be fine. You can see him soon." the officer replied.

I picked up a few clothes, and left with the officer. On the way there, the officer was quiet.

"Why do I have to go to a facility and stay?" I asked.

"It's just temporarily while we figure out what happened to your brother." He replied.

"Why can't I just stay with Daddy?" I asked.

"Because we are not sure if it's safe for you to be in your father's care right now." The officer replied.

"Why wouldn't it be safe?" I asked. *"Daddy has never hurt anyone. He might be mean sometimes, but he wouldn't hurt a fly."*

"Pepper, everything will be fine. Don't worry about anything. We will get all this sorted out in time." the officer replied.

We arrived where I was going to be staying at. It was a big building on the outside with a lot of windows. Inside were rooms full of beds. The building contained all girls, about my age or a little older. The lady that worked there was really nice to me. She showed me where I would be sleeping.

"What is your name child?" She asked.

"Pepper." I replied.

"Pepper? Now where did you get a name like that?" She asked sarcastically.

"That's just what my mommy uses to call me." I

replied back.*" She got sick and died. We been living with Daddy, but my brother takes care of me most of the time. I think my brother ran away. But he will come back for me. We are going to go on a trip together. He is just out getting things together for our trip. He is going to be upset though when he finds out that they took his book. We will have to get it back before we leave...*"

"My child-- Pepper, you have had a long day it seems. Why don't you lay down and rest. Let the police figure things out. Everything will be fine." She sweetly said.

"What about school?" I asked.

"We have our own school here." She replied.

"What about my friends?" I asked.

"You will make new friends. Now rest my child." She replied softly as she walked out the door.

I was still confused as to why I couldn't stay with Frank. Surely, I didn't want to go to a new school or make new friends. I just wanted Red to come back to get me so we could go home. Resting in my new bed, I gazed around at the other girls in the room. Some were up wandering around the room quietly while others were sleeping. I spoke softly to a girl next to me.

"Why do we have to stay in our rooms?" I asked.

This is our quiet break. We get one every day right before lunch. When the food is cooked, they will come get all of us." the girl replied.

"Who?" I asked.

"Miss Drake and Miss Keener. They always come in when lunch is ready. You can sleep if you want." said the girl.

"No. I don't want to sleep. I just want to go home." I softly replied.

"Why are you here?" She asked.

"I was brought here until the police find my brother. They wouldn't let me stay with my daddy. Do you think my daddy will come visit me here?" I said.

"No. we don't get outside visitors here unless you are being adopted out. That's not too often though." the girl replied.

"Well, my brother will come get me soon. I won't be here long." I replied.

"Don't get your hopes up--" she said as she tried to figure out what to call me.

"Pepper, that's my name." I replied.

"My name is Mae. Nice to meet you Pepper, but like I said, don't get your hopes up for nothing around here." Mae replied.

"Whatever." I thought to my myself as I rolled the other way.

My stomach growled with hunger. I hadn't eaten all day. Moments later, a woman entered the room to let us know it was lunch time. Everyone walked over to line up in front of the woman, so I followed. I stood behind Mae asking her questions.

"Who is that?" I quietly asked.

"That is Miss Keener. The woman who brought you in earlier was Miss Drake."

We filed down the hallway to the cafeteria area in a

single line. No one spoke on the way. After entering the cafeteria, we each grabbed a tray and was seated at a table. We were allowed to speak quietly to each other while we ate.

I plopped down next to Mae at the table. Another girl beside us started crying.

"Who is she?" I asked in curiosity.

"That's Charlie. She was dropped off here a few years ago. Her daddy went missing a few years back. Paul was his name, I think. Yeah." Mae replied.

"Paul?" I confusedly asked.

"Yes. That was his name. Charlie's cousin Cherry was murdered by her daddy is what I heard. I guess that's when Paul came up missing. He probably couldn't handle the news about his niece. No other family could be tracked down, so they brought Charlie here." replied Mae.

"Wait! Her daddy isn't missing. I see him on my way to the library one day. I talked to him." I said.

"You couldn't have talked to him. If he isn't missing then why hasn't he came to get Charlie?" Mae asked.

"I don't know. He seemed like a caring person. I don't understand why he would do something like that." I replied.

We finished eating, then went out to play. A few weeks went by before the police officer came back to talk to me.

"Have you found my brother?" I asked desperately.

"No, we haven't." the officer sighed.

"Where's my father? I want to go home!" I demanded.

"Pepper, you can't go home yet. After thoroughly reading Red's book, we had to arrest your daddy." the officer sadly said.

"Arrest? But why?" I asked.

"We think he had something to do with Red's disappearance."

"What do you mean?" I asked in anger.

"We can't go into anymore details right now. You are going to have to stay here a little longer until we can contact your family to come get you. I would like to ask you a few more questions."

"He wouldn't do this." I replied.

"Pepper, has your daddy ever hit you?" The officer *asked.*

"No! Most certainly not." I angrily said.

"Have you ever seen him hit your brother?" The *officer continued.*

"No." I replied.

"So, you have never seen your daddy get angry at all?" the officer asked.

"I have seen him mad a few times, but he has never hit anyone." I replied confused.

"Can you remember back when your mom was alive Pepper? asked the officer.

"Yes. I remember a lot of things. Happy moments mostly." I replied.

"Do you ever remember your dad cooking for your mom?" The officer asked.

"Yes, he did all the time after she got sick. Maybe a few

times before that. Why do you ask that?" I asked confused.

"Just trying to confirm a few things. I will come back another time if I need to ask you anything else." The officer replied.

"Wait! I wanted to ask you something. Is there a missing man named Paul?" I asked out of curiosity.

"Paul who?" the officer asked.

"I don't know his last name. His daughter is here. Charlie." I replied.

"That was a case from a few years ago." the officer said.

"He's not missing. I see him not too long ago. We talked about Cherry." I exclaimed to the officer.

"Pepper, you are not making any sense." said the officer with a confused look on his face. *"Paul is dead. We found his remains a few months after he went missing. We just never had the heart to tell Charlie about it. He took the loss of his niece Cherry hard, and we think he went off to kill himself out of guilt because he knew she was being abused.*

They were really close. Charlie had just moved in with Paul after her mother died of a sudden heart attack. Paul had never seen his daughter till then."

"*That's not possible. I sat and talked with Paul. We held hands. He told me the story about Cherry and he said no one knew. He --" I tried to explain.*

"*Stop Pepper! You must be mistaken with someone else."* the officer firmly said.

"*But I'm not mistaken officer. I see and talked to him."* I replied sadly.

"*Pepper, I am leaving now. If you can remember anything else about your father or Red, let miss Keener know and she will contact me to come back out." The officer replied.*

Miss Keener escorted me back to my room. I had a hard time understanding why the officer didn't believe me about Paul. The more I thought about it, the angrier I became. I had the idea that when I left this facility, I would go find Paul. That way the police could see I was telling the truth. He would be forced to believe me if he saw Paul in person.

I went to bed after dinner searching for answers in my

mind that I knew weren't there. I had trouble believing that Frank could hurt anyone. There were no reasons in my mind I could find as to why he would possibly want to hurt his own son. The police had to be mistaken. Everything that had gone on in my life was too overwhelming for me to handle.

Chapter 5

Later that night, I found myself tossing and turning trying to sleep. Mae was awake too. Every time I glanced over; she was staring at me.

"Why are you looking at me like that?" I asked.

"What did the police say? Did they find your brother?" Mae asked.

"No. But they arrested my daddy. They think he had something to do with my brother's disappearance. They were asking me bunch of questions. Before they left, I asked them about Charlie's daddy." I replied.

"You did? What did they say?" Mae quickly asked.

"They said her daddy is dead. They found his remains a few months after his disappearance. They just haven't told Charlie yet, so don't say anything. I told him that Paul wasn't dead, and that I had just talked to him about Cherry's death." I replied.

"Pepper, have you ever seen dead people before?"

Mae asked.

"I'm telling you he wasn't dead. He was a person, like you and me." I said.

"Think about it Pepper. What if he was dead, and the police did find his remains? That means you were talking to his ghost." *Mae explained.*

Being quiet the rest of the night, I wandered if any of it could be true. If Paul were really dead, then why would he come to me? With unknown answers, I was hoping to one day find out. Confusion took over my life, and where things would go from there. I finally fell asleep a few hours before dawn.

The next day, I pretended to be sick so I could sleep half the day. I stayed to myself all evening, then went back to bed that night. Still confused, I didn't want to be bothered by anyone. I visualized about Red's return for me until I fell asleep.

I awakened early the next morning. Most of the other girls were still sleeping.

Slowly, I made me to a window near the corner of the

room. While watching as people walked by the facility, I had hoped I would see Paul so the police would believe me, but there was no sign of Paul anywhere. I remained at the window until we were called for breakfast.

While eating, Mae struck up a conversation with me.

*"Pepper, did you think about what I said the other night to you?" S*he asked.

"A little." I replied.

"So, do you think you are seeing ghosts?" She asked curiously.

"I don't know Mae. I'm feeling confused about everything right now. Just leave me alone." I replied.

Mae didn't speak through the rest of breakfast. After awhile of being in the facility, depression started to overcome me. It was the same routine everyday at the facility; breakfast, schooling, quiet break, lunch, play time, homework, dinner, and bed. I became miserable there. Home was where I wanted to be home. I couldn't comprehend why Red would promise to take care of me, then take off without a trace. He didn't even take his stuff and left his book behind. If only he would have been open with me about what was going on, I could have known how to help. Red being secretive never helped our relationship.

Not a lot of girls associated with me at the facility. I hung out with Mae, but she annoyed me sometimes with the ghost talks even though I try not to show it. I isolate myself a lot. Mae had me thinking almost everyday about the ghost stuff. I really didn't know what to believe.

"What if I am seeing ghosts? Is it such a bad thing? They seem so real though. What if half of these girls in here that I am seeing now are ghosts?" "And if I was seeing ghosts, then why haven't I seen my Mom?"

I questioned if anything in my life was real at that moment. Not wanting to be around anyone, I had asked to go to Miss Keener's office where I stayed most of the day.

"Miss Keener, are you a ghost?" I asked.

"Can you touch me?" She asked back quickly.

"Yes." I replied.

"Then I am not a ghost." She explained.

"But I held hands with Paul, and I think he was a ghost. The police said they found his remains, but he was real to me." I said.

"Pepper, I don't think you are seeing ghosts. I think-- I think you were talking to someone else, and you thought it was Paul." Miss Keener explained.

"I wasn't." I replied.

"Let's get you some dinner now before you go to bed." She replied.

We went to the cafeteria to eat. After we ate, Miss Keener escorted me to my room for the night. The racing thoughts in my mind kept me awake.

"Where have you been all day?" asked Mae.

"I was in Miss Keener's office." I replied.

"Were you in trouble?" Mae asked curiously.

"No. I wanted to be there." I replied.

"Why?" Mae asked.

"Because I just did. We talked about some things." I

69

RAELYN SHAYE

said.

"What did you talk about?" She asked.

"Look, stop asking me questions Mae." I angrily said.

For a moment, I realized my brother Red was coming out of me again. Now I know how he probably felt when I asked him a lot of questions. Maybe that's why he took off and never came back for me. He was probably annoyed with my questioning, and decided to take the trip on his own. This is all my fault. He might not ever come back for me now.

A few months went by without a word from the police.

"Miss Keener, Why hasn't the police came back for me yet?" I asked.

*"They are still investigating things. You will have to give them more time." S*he replied.

"How much time?" I asked in curiosity.

"I don't know. Investigations can sometimes take awhile." said Miss Keener.

"Why do they take so long?" I asked in disappointment.

"They have to have time to look everything over. It shouldn't take much longer." She explained.

Eventually, I felt more comfortable with my stay at the facility, but still defiant in my mind about the same daily routines. Mae and I ended up becoming best friends. She introduced me to more of the girls we lived with. I had good grades in school also.

"Pepper, you are a smart girl I see." said Miss Drake.

"Thank you." I replied as I smiled.

"What do you want to be when you grow up?" She asked.

"I don't know. I have never thought about it." I replied.

"Well, you should probably start thinking about your life." Miss Drake said.

"Why?" I asked. *"I Still have a long time before I grow up."*

"Pepper, it's never too early to think about your future." She stated.

71

Almost instantly, I refused to think about my future. I felt there would be plenty of time to decide what I wanted to be when I grew up.

As I lay in bed at night thinking about Red, I missed him taking care of me everyday. Basically, I had lost my whole family. Isabelle died, Frank was in jail, and Red ran away. No other family members stepped up to take me in yet. I had come to the conclusion that I would have to live at the facility until I became old enough to be on my own.

"Maybe you were right Mae." I said.

"Right about what?" She asked.

"When I first came here, you told me not to get my hopes up about leaving. "I replied.

"I'm sorry Pepper." Mae sadly said.

"No, I should have listened to you. I will never get out of here." I said with disappointment.

"You might Pepper. Maybe they will find someone to keep you." She said.

"No Mae. I have been here for months. If someone

wanted me, they would have come to get me already." I replied.

"Don't get your hopes down just yet. You never know, anything could happen at this point." Mae said.

"You can say that again." I quietly said to myself.

"Come on, let's go eat some lunch." Mae said.

After lunch, we raced outside to play. I noticed some construction men were working on a fence at the side of the facility. As the other girls played, I sat to watch the men.

"Pepper. Come play with us." Mae said.

"No. I don't want to." I replied.

What's wrong Pepper?" She asked.

"Nothing. I just want to sit here awhile." I said.

"Okay, have fun then." said Mae as she ran back to the playground.

I glanced over and saw that the construction men were on break. They left the big hole in the fence unattended. While Miss drake was over on the other side of the grounds watching the others play, I quietly inched my way over to the fence line beside the hole. I knew it would be easy to sneak out of the fence. I waited a few minutes longer. When no one was paying attention, I squeezed through the hole of the fence.

I ran down the road as fast as I could. As I approached the cities' big park, I saw a bench to rest on. It surprised me that no one had noticed me leaving the facility grounds.

I nervously waited for someone to notice where I had come from, but no one did. Everyone was busy, going about their day. It wouldn't be long before the facility figured out, I was gone. I wasn't sure where to go, so I found my way to the house I lived in previously. After I arrived to my old house, I stood in front of the door debating on whether to open it. As I slowly reached my hand out in front of me, the door came flying open. I fell backward in fear.

"What are you doing?" a man asked.

"Uhh-- nothing sir." I stuttered.

"Then why are you here?" He asked.

"I-- I use to live here." I hesitantly replied.

"Well, you don't live here no more." He said.

"I didn't know. I thought maybe my daddy still lived here." I explained.

"Who's your daddy?" the man asked.

"Frank." I replied.

"Frank? You mean the guy that's in jail?" He asked.

"Yes. I didn't know he was still in jail sir. I thought he came back here." I replied.

"I hear he isn't getting out anytime soon child." the man said.

"You hear?" I asked.

"Yes. Word on the streets are that he did something to his son. He is going to be locked away for the rest of his life. Hey, aren't you supposed to be at some kind of facility?" He asked.

"Yes. I ran away from there. I don't like it there." I replied.

"What is your name child?" He asked.

75

"Pepper." I replied.

"Well Pepper, you know I will have to take you back." the man firmly said.

"No!" I yelled as I ran away from him.

I returned to the park area to find somewhere to go for awhile so no one would see me. The decision was quickly made to go to the big hills where Red and I use to go sledding. On my way there, I noticed people staring at me. Nervously, I ran the rest of the way. After getting to the hills, I relaxed for awhile in the grass. There, I saw a small wooded area with a bunch of trees behind the hills, so I went to hide in the woods.

Darkness approached as I tried to find a tree to hide in. I noticed a tree that had a platform on the branches. It must have been someone's tree house they tried to build, but I didn't care as long as it was a place for me to hide. After climbing the tree to settle on the platform, I watched the sun set and debated on whether to give up and return to the facility. I knew I wouldn't survive out in the woods for long by myself. No plans of where I would go or how I would live were ever made. In deep thought, I ended up falling asleep right after dark.

Hours later, I was awakened a few hours later by the sounds of footsteps. I was too frightened to move. My heart raced as the footsteps came closer. I heard sticks cracking and braking with each step.

"What if someone else stays in this tree?" I thought to myself. *"What am I going to say if someone catches me up here?"*

All of a sudden, the stepping sounds stopped beneath me. I became as still as a mouse as I held my breath and waited for the moment someone would reach up to grab me from below, but nothing happened. After a few more minutes, I calmly glanced over the platform to see who was there. It was so dark in the woods, that I could barely see my hands in front of my face. I became terrified and shaken.

As I looked toward the ground beneath me, I noticed movement in the darkness. It looked as if someone was sitting against the tree. I wasn't sure what to do or say, but I knew if I were caught, I would be in trouble. Wandering who could be watching me as the shadows moved below, I eventually decided I had to take my chances to find out. I was cold and hungry anyway, so it wouldn't have hurt me to be sent back to the facility.

"Who's there?" I whispered quietly.

There was no answer. I didn't know if whoever it was heard me, so I spoke up a little louder.

"Who's there." I whispered loudly.

Crunch! Crackle! and Pop! Went the leaves and sticks below me. I saw a big shadow of an animal quickly run away. The dark night gave me no determination of what type of animal it was? I experienced heavy breathing as my heart beat quickly. I wanted to run straight back to the facility, but I was too frightened to leave the tree. I eventually calmed myself down, and fell back to sleep.

The next morning, I woke up shivering. It wasn't as cool during the day as it was at night. I observed around the woods from the platform before climbing out of the tree and hurried back toward the city on the hunt for food. As I approached a store, I noticed a missing person sign hung on the store's window. My picture and name were on the sign.

I turned around quickly to walk away, but a police

officer was standing behind me. Then, I stood in front of him in fear. He saw that I was the missing child on the sign and put me in his cop car to take me back to the facility. On the way, the officer continually glanced at me through his rear-view mirror.

"Everyone's been worried about you. Where have you been?" He asked.

I refused to answer him and had no intention to talk to him as I held my head downward most of the way to the facility. In a way, I was happy to go back. It was a scary short-lived experience being out on my own. I imagined what kind of trouble I would be in once I returned to the facility.

"Am I going to be in trouble for running away?" I asked the officer.

"You're not in trouble, but you're lucky to be alive. Do you realize how many missing children reports we get? We never thought we would see you again." He replied.

"I was only gone overnight." I replied.

The officer never responded. He might have been right. Maybe I was lucky to be alive, after last night's scare. I was happy it turned out to be an animal.

Chapter 6

We had finally returned to the facility and the officer escorted me in. Miss Keener met me at the locked doors inside.

"Dear child, where have you been?" Miss Keener asked as she hugged me. *"Don't you know it's dangerous wandering off by yourself? We have been up all night worried about you."*

"I'm sorry." I softly said.

"Thank you for bringing her back officer. Come on Pepper, let's go to my office to talk for awhile." Miss Keener said.

We walked to her office together. I sat down slowly as Miss Keener closed the office door.

"What in the world was going through your mind Pepper?" asked Miss Keener.

"I just wanted to leave." I replied.

"You left through that hole in the fence, didn't you?"

*S*he asked.

"*Yes.*" I softly replied.

"*Where did you stay last night?*" She asked curiously.

"*I stayed in the woods, on the other side of the hills.*" I replied.

"*You are lucky to be sitting here right now Pepper. I want you to promise me that you won't do anything like this again!*" She said in a worried voice.

"*I promise.*" I sighed.

Miss Keener let me eat breakfast in her office. After I ate, she sent me to my room.

"*I want you to stay in here and rest until lunch.*" *S*he said.

"*Okay.*" I replied.

I fell to sleep in my bed for awhile. Mae woke me up right before lunch.

"*Where have you been?*" asked Mae.

"I don't want to talk about it right now Mae." I replied.

*"You had the whole facility talking about your disappearance. We thought we were never going to see you again." S*he said.

No reply was made back to her. Everyone stared at me during lunch, so I tried not to look up at anyone. When lunch was finished, I had to go do school work while the other girls went out to play. In time, I finished my work, ate dinner later that day, and went to bed. I knew I would be safe here for the night.

The next morning, Miss Keener awakened me.

"Pepper. Wake up. Someone is here to see you." She said happily.

"Is it my brother?" I softly asked.

"No. Come with me." She replied.

I followed behind her closely as we entered a private room, where I had to wait while she went to get my visitor. Anxiously, I sat wandering who could it be. A few minutes went by before the door finally opened. The police officer from Frank's case had come to visit me. I thought I was going to be punished for running away. My heart raced as I had determined they were going to put me in jail. He walked toward me to sit in front of me.

"Are you going to arrest me?" I asked.

"No. Why would I arrest you?" replied the officer.

"Because I ran away from here."I said.

"No, Pepper. I am here for another reason." The *officer said dreadfully.*

"Have you found my brother?" I asked in curiosity.

"Yes, we have." H*e* sadly replied.

"Where is he? Can I see him?" I excitedly asked.

"No. Pepper, we found Red's body near a creek by the woods right outside the city over the hills a week ago." explained the Officer.

"What do you mean you found his body?" I slowly asked.

"Your brother is dead Pepper." The Officer replied.

"No! It's not true!" I angrily yelled.

"Pepper, we are very sorry, but it is true. Funeral arrangements are being made. One of our officers will escort you to Red's funeral, so you can be there. I will let you know when it's going to be." He explained.

"How did he die?" I asked.

"It looks as if he was strangulated. The autopsy will tell more." He replied.

"Who would want to hurt Red?" I asked. *"He was a nice person."*

"We don't know yet. We are still investigating. When we find out more, I will let you know." The Officer explained.

In disbelief, I speechlessly cried at what I was hearing. First, I lost Isabelle, and now I had lost Red. My feelings were very hostile inside. I wanted to strangle whoever had hurt Red.

"Pepper, you can stay in here for awhile if you need to." Miss Keener said.

"What's going to happen with me now?" I asked.

"Let's not worry about that right now Pepper. You will be taken care of." She replied.

I remained in the private room for awhile longer, then sadly went about my day. A few days later, I had another visit from the police.

"Do you know when the funeral is?" I asked the police officer.

"Yes. It will be in two days." He replied.

"Did you find out who killed Red?" I asked.

"Pepper, we are charging your father for the murder of Red." He replied.

"What?" I shockingly asked.

"We have evidence that points to your father." replied the Officer.

"Frank wouldn't do something like this. He has never hurt anyone." I explained.

"Pepper, there are going to be things said in court that you probably might not want to know about." The Officer

claimed.

"What kind of things?" I asked confused.

"Well, things about your mother, father, and Red." He replied.

"I already know everything about them." I said confused.

"No pepper, I don't think you are aware of half the things that went on in your house." The officer explained.

"Then tell me what I don't know." I smartly stated.

"That will come soon. I just wanted you to know, you might not like some of the things that come out against your father." He replied.

"Can I come to court to watch?" I asked.

"No. court isn't a place for little girls. You may have to come testify, but other than that you will not be allowed in the court room." He replied.

"How will I know what is said against Frank?" I asked.

"News gets around fast Pepper. It will eventually get

back to you. If you have any questions about anything you hear, you can call us." He explained.

The day of Red's funeral had arrived. The news had done spread about the discovery of Red's body, so I expected a lot of people to be there. The police officer came to escort me to the funeral. On the way, not a word was spoken to each other. We pulled up to a big church, where Red's body had been laid out. There were dozens of people swarming the outside of the church.

"Who are all these people?" I asked the Officer.

"People who live in the community. They came to offer support." He replied.

"Why aren't they inside?" I asked curiously.

"There isn't room for everyone inside. Just those who are family and close friends are allowed inside. Everyone else will stand outside to show their support to the family." He replied.

"Is my dad here?" I asked.

"No. he is in jail. He was not allowed to come today."

replied the Officer.

"Why not?" I asked.

"Pepper, when someone is accused of killing another person, they don't get to go to the funeral." He replied.

"But what if you're wrong? What if my dad didn't kill my brother?" I asked angrily.

"We have plenty enough evidence that proves otherwise Pepper." He replied.

"I would like to know what." I mumbled under my breath as I got out of the car.

As I fought through the crowd of people, I heard someone from a distance holler my name. I glanced around, but I didn't recognize anyone. Soon as I reached the door to the church at the top of the steps, I heard my name again and quickly turned around to look. I could not believe it! Candy was trying to push her way through people to get to me so I leaped off the steps toward her.

"Candy!" I yelled as I ran to her.

"Pepper!" She yelled back. *"Where have you been?"*

"The police are making me stay at a facility right now." I replied.

"When will you get out?" Candy asked.

"I don't know. Hopefully soon." I replied.

"Alright young lady. Let's go. We need to get inside the church." the officer said as he approached me from behind.

As I entered the church and proceeded toward the casket Red was in, I noticed the casket was closed so I turned to the officer for answers.

"Why is Red's casket closed?" I asked the officer.

"His body was badly decomposed, so we didn't want it open for the funeral." He replied.

"Decomposed?" I asked confused.

"Yes. After someone dies, there body starts rotting away." the Officer replied.

"Can I see in the casket after the funeral?" I asked.

"No Pepper. I want you to remember your brother the way he used to be. We don't need you having bad dreams of

*rotting bodies." H*e replied.

I sat next to the officer waiting on the funeral to start. My aunts, uncles, and cousins were sitting on the other side of the church. They were whispering to each other as they stared at me. I also seen some old friends of Isabelle and few others I didn't know. After a few minutes, an old lady approached me.

*"How are you, Pepper?" T*he lady asked as she smiled.

"I am fine, thank you." I politely replied back.

"You look just like your father." She said.

"You know Frank?" I asked.

"Yes, I do. He is my son." She replied.

"Your son?" I asked confused.

"Yes. We haven't spoken in years. It's a shame we had to meet up at such a time as this." the lady replied sadly.

"You can't be his mother. His mother died in a car accident." I said.

"Is that what he told you child?" She asked.

"Yes. That's why I never knew them." I replied.

"Pepper, I didn't die in a car accident. We had a lot of problems out of Frank. Raising him wasn't easy. He stayed in trouble with the law. One day, he had a fallen out with his father. He left town and we never heard from him again. His father eventually passed away and I have been living on my own. I seen Frank's picture on the television, and here I am. I always wandered if I had any grandchildren out there somewhere."

With an astonished look on my face, I didn't know how to reply to the old woman.

She finally took her seat as the funeral started. The funeral wasn't long. A few people spoke of happy times they had with Red. The officer asked me if I wanted to speak, but I refused. After the funeral, we were escorted to the graveyard. Everyone gathered around Red's casket to say their goodbye's. Red was being buried next to Isabelle. I was allowed to stay for awhile afterward to visit her grave. I was full of sadness and confusion. It was hard to grasp what was happening in my life. The officer drove me back to the facility. On the way, I questioned him.

"Was that old lady really Frank's mother?" I asked.

"I am not sure. That is something we are currently checking in to." The Officer replied.

"That would make her my grandma, right?" I asked.

"Yes. It would, if it's true." He replied.

"Do you believe Frank use to get in trouble with the law?" I asked.

"We are investigating that also." He replied.

After he dropped me off at the facility, I sadly continued my day. Hopefully, I wouldn't be stuck at the facility the rest of my childhood. Curiosity haunted me as to why Frank would do something this horrible, if it were true. Also, I wanted to know why he would lie about his parents. I bothered Miss Keener until I convinced her to ask the police if I could have a visit with my father before his trial started. The police agreed to let me visit Frank, but they had to monitor the whole conversation. I was confused about it, but I agreed.

I arrived at the prison where Frank was being held.

Miss Keener was kind enough to take me. The police escorted me to a room where I waited awhile. They said I would be on the other side of the bars, so Frank couldn't touch me. Even though I was a little afraid, I just wanted answers. The police finally brought Frank in. As I walked over to talk to him, he held his head down in disappointment.

"Hi daddy." I said, but there was no reply. *"Daddy, are all these things true that the police are saying? Did you kill Red?"* I asked, but still no reply. *"I went to Red's funeral. I met an old lady who claimed she was your mom. I thought your mom was dead. Is your mom dead daddy?"* I asked as he slowly started to lift his head.

"Who is this woman you speak of?" Frank asked.

"I don't know. She said she was your mother. She said how bad you were as a child, and that you got into some kind of fight with your dad. She said you left town and she never heard from you again. She seen your picture on the television and came to Red's funeral." I explained.

"Don't listen to her Pepper. Whatever she says isn't true. She is just a crazy old lady. You stay away from her." Frank said.

"The police said they were checking into everything she told me." I stated.

"I said stay away from her! I am done talking! Leave now Pepper" Frank yelled angrily.

"But I don't want to leave. I want to know who the old woman is, and if you were the one that killed Red." I said.

"Pepper, leave right now." Frank said firmly with an evil look.

Suddenly, I became so frightened that I practically ran out. I had never seen such an evil look come from Frank before. It was like he wasn't the same person I knew before. I couldn't comprehend what had changed in him. Even though I didn't get the answers I was looking for, I got to see another side of my father that I didn't know. Maybe that old woman was his mother, and Frank was bad all the time. I began to wander if there were anymore surprises in my life I hadn't ran into yet.

On our way back to the facility, Miss Keener tried to comfort me.

"Don't be upset Pepper. Everything will work out for

the best. " Miss Keener said.

"How did daddy become so evil? " I asked.

"What do you mean by evil? " She asked.

"Just the way he looked at me when he scared me off." I replied.

"He was just angry. I am sure he didn't mean to scare you. " She stated.

"I have never seen him like that Miss Keener.

When we arrived at the facility, my older cousin Daisy was awaiting my return.

"What are you doing here Daisy? " I asked.

"I came to visit you. How have you been Pepper? " She asked.

"Good I guess. " I replied.

"You guess? " She asked with a smirk.

"How would you be if you lost your family Daisy? " I asked sarcastically.

"Not good. So, I hear Frank killed your brother. I always knew there was something weird about him." Daisy stated.

"If you came here to start trouble, there's the door." I replied as I pointed toward the exit.

"I didn't come for trouble Pepper." She replied.

"Then what did you come for?" I asked.

"I was talking to my mom after the funeral. She seems to think it might be good for you to live out on the island with her. She's getting older, and could use a little help now that we are all grown and have moved off." She explained.

"I don't want to go there. Why don't you move back there and help your mom?" I asked.

"Pepper, I am grown now. I have a life of my own. The only life you have, is this facility." She replied.

"Go away Daisy!" I yelled as I ran to my room crying.

I felt confused about why Daisy came to visit with a bad attitude. We had always gotten along before. Just because she wanted me to go live with her mom, didn't mean I was going to. Wherever I end up, will be my choice. I wish I were old enough to live by myself. I didn't want others making me do things I didn't want to do.

Chapter 7

Weeks later, the police visited to let me know that Frank had pleaded not guilty to the murder of Red. He was set to go on trial within a few months. The police were getting their evidence together, while waiting for the trial to begin. They also mentioned the old lady at the funeral.

"The old lady you met at the funeral was confirmed to be Frank's mother. That means, she is your grandma Pepper." The officer said.

"Why would my daddy keep it a secret?" I asked.

"Well, we also investigated the allegations she made about your father, and found that she was telling the truth. I think he may have moved to start a new life, and tried to avoid going back to his old ways of living." He stated.

"Will I get to visit her sometime?" I asked.

"Actually, she talked with us about you coming to live with her for a while." He said.

"I don't know her that well. I'm not sure if I want to do

that." I said.

"*No one is going to make you go anywhere if you don't want to Pepper. You can stay here for as long as you would like. When you are comfortable, you can make the choice to live with your grandma.*" The Officer said.

"*What if she doesn't like me?*" I asked.

"*She will like you. As a matter of fact, she talked about how sweet you were. She is excited to know she has a granddaughter. She wants to get to know you Pepper.*" The officer replied.

"*I will think about it, and let you know.*" I said.

I rested in bed dwelling on everything the officer said to me. I saw another part of Frank that I never knew about. If I went to live with my grandma, I could find out more about Frank's dark side. I wasn't sure if I should know, but I knew I wanted to know.

"*What are you thinking about Pepper?*" Mae asked.

"*Some decision I have to make.*" I replied.

"*Decision?*" She asked.

"Yeah. My grandma wants me to come live with her." I replied.

"That's exciting news!" She whispered with excitement.

"I don't know if I want to." I said.

"Why not?" She asked confused.

"I am scared, I guess. I don't really know her. My dad kept her a secret from me." I explained. *"What if I'm not happy there?"*

"I am sure they won't make you stay if you are not happy. I'm not sure why your dad didn't tell you about her, but you should go try it. You may like it there. It has to be better than this place anyway." Mae replied.

"I know. I am just confused about it all right now." I said.

"I know it has to be a hard decision to make, but you will make up your mind soon. Just sleep on it." She stated.

Since I never received the chance to visit with my grandma on Frank's side, I knew it would be awkward for me at first, but that would eventually fade as time passed. I had so much to take in, I felt overwhelmed as I tossed in my bed. After a few hours of reasoning, I finally fell asleep.

In the following weeks, I couldn't help but realize the trial would soon begin for Frank and had wished that I could be there somehow. Even though the police had all their evidence, I still had this sense of belief that Frank was innocent. A bad dream was what I was hoping all of this was, and I would wake up at any moment. I went from a life full of happiness, to a life full of sadness in a matter of a few years. Miss Keener was there when I needed to ease my mind. She could be nice, and take me to the trial.

"I want to be at the trial when it starts." I stated to Miss Keener.

"Pepper, you know what the police officer said about that." She replied.

"But it's my daddy. Why can't I be there?" I asked.

"Court isn't a place for little kids." She replied.

"I'm not a baby you know." I said.

"Yes, I know. But you are still young, and you don't need to be exposed to that kind of trial." She stated.

"Can I just sneak in?" I asked. *"I don't have to stay for the whole hearing."*

"No. the police will keep you updated on everything that's happening." She replied.

I had grown fed up of living the facility life and wanted to leave to go live more freely. One part of me knew my aunt needed me to come stays with her on the island. It was a beautiful place from what I could recall. I was very young when Isabelle took me there, so I don't remember much. I wasn't sure if there were many other kids to play with, or if there were many things to do on the island.

Another part of me really wanted to know Frank's mom. Once again, curiosity had me wandering what kind of person she was like. She didn't appear to be a bad person, but then I wasn't sure about anything anymore. It was frightening for me to dwell about it. I wasn't sure I could leave if I had decided I didn't like living with my grandma, but needed to figure out something soon. Summer was approaching, and I didn't want to stay at the facility with no freedom. The decision of where to go became difficult for me to make.

I finally decided to go outside with the other girls for the first time since I ran away. Miss Drake gawked me down, even though the fence was fixed now. I watched the other girls play. For some reason, I wasn't feeling up to doing anything. It was a bit warmer out and I was anxious for summer to arrive.

"You should come jump rope with us." She said.

"I will some other time." I replied.

"I know you got a lot going on Pepper, but you have to keep living life." She said.

"I am living life Mae. I am here, aren't I?" I asked.

"Yes, but all you do is sit around depressed. You need to live life. Get up and do things. Forget about what is going on with the trial for awhile." Mae replied.

"You don't understand Mae. I can't just forget about what is going on right now." I said.

"I do understand Pepper. I was abuse by my parents when I was younger. They were on a lot of drugs. I went

104

hungry most days. They hit on me and--" she said as she hesitated.

"I'm sorry Mae. I didn't know. You don't have to tell me anything else." I explained.

"My point is, I had to learn to leave it behind me and move on." She continued.

"I can try. Come on, let's go jump rope." I said as I smiled.

We jumped rope and played together before returning inside. Maybe Mae had a point. I should figure out how to move on from all the bad things in my life. She was a few years older than me, so she had to be smarter. I desired to find peace in my life to heal from the pain I was feeling. The more I thought about it, the more I knew I had to make my decision about moving. Since the only grandma I knew was from Isabelle's side, I leaned more toward getting to know the grandma I never visited. I decided I should speak to the officer for advice. Maybe he could help me make my decision about where to live.

The police were busy with court approaching. I tried

my best to find the peace of mind I needed to move on. I had to find a way to keep myself busy. It was going to be hard for me to do being at the facility. The continuous daily routine was boring to me. It wasn't my kind of life. Each day that passed, I became more anxious. There had been no more visits from the police officer. I decided to harass Miss Keener about driving me to the station. She agreed to take me so I could talk to the officer again. On the way to the station, Miss Keener tried to figure out my reason for wanting to go, but I wouldn't tell her anything. Curious about the trial, since it was closely approaching, I debated if I should leave the decision about moving alone until after the trial.

After arriving at the police station, Miss Keener helped me find the officer from Frank's case. I was escorted to his office, where I waited until the officer came back. Miss Keener remained patiently at the front desk for me to get finished. As I waited, my curiosity arose once again. I noticed big file cabinets in the room with me. The front of them were labeled with alphabet letters. From what I had learned in school, the letters were to represent the beginning letter of your last name.

By this point, my curiosity had hit me extremely hard,

and I couldn't resist the temptation of exploring. I found the letter of my last name and opened the drawer to see file folders with first names listed. As I went through the names, I came across Frank, Red, and my name. I glanced through the folder with my name on it first. It had information about myself and where I was staying. Then, I quickly put my folder back to grab Red's folder. As I searched through Red's folder, I saw copies of pages the police had made from his diary book. Suddenly, I heard talking outside the office door so I grabbed the diary pages and quickly stuffed them in my pants. The folder was thrown back into the cabinet as I sat down just in time before the officer walked in.

"Good morning, Pepper." The Officer said.

"Morning." I quickly replied.

"Is something wrong?" He asked.

"No! I uhh-- I just wanted to talk to you about something, but I am not feeling well now." I replied hesitantly.

"You are already here. What did you need to talk about?" The officer asked with a confused look.

"I was just having a hard time deciding where to move.

My older cousin came to visit me. She said mt aunt needed me to go stay with her on the island, but you told me my grandma wants me to stay with her." I replied.

"Pepper, I can't tell you who to go live with. You are going to have to make that decision on your own." The Officer stated.

"I was thinking about going to live with my grandma." I said.

"You have plenty of time to make that decision. We weren't going to push anything right now with the trial days away. I know how hard everything is for you right now." The Officer replied.

"I want to move before summer comes." I said.

"Then I can set it up for your grandma to come pick you up at the facility." The Officer stated.

"What if I get there, and decide I don't like it?" I asked.

"If you don't like it then you contact me, and I will come get you Pepper." The Officer replied.

"Okay. I will try it with my grandma then." I said.

"It will take some time for me to set things up. I will start the procedures today. It has to be approved through the court, but I will do what I can to rush things." he said.

"Okay." I replied.

He sent me back to the facility with Miss Keener. After returning, I had lunch with the other girls, then went to my room because I didn't want to go outside. Then, I removed the copies of Red's pages I had taken from his folder at the station. My mind wandered where the rest of his book was. I didn't understand why the police would only keep certain pages of it, but I knew I would be in trouble if they found out I took the copies from the station. I wished to have gotten the chance to look through Frank's folder. Maybe it had contained something about the upcoming trial. I couldn't return to see, that would definitely be risky.

The other girls returned to the room before I could start reading Red's pages. It was raining, so Miss Drake wouldn't allow them play outside. I hid the pages until I had the chance to read them alone and sat in deep thought staring out the window of the facility.

"Are you okay Pepper?" Mae asked.

109

"Yes." I sighed.

"Where were you earlier?" She asked.

"I went to the police station with Miss Keener." I replied.

"What for?" Mae asked with curiosity.

"I talked to the officer about moving, I am going to go live with my grandma for awhile." I replied.

"I'm happy for you, but I will miss you" Mae stated sadly.

"Maybe you can come for visits Mae." I stated.

"I don't think they will let me, but you could come here to see me, Pepper." She replied.

"Yeah, I will do that." I said.

After eating dinner, I went straight to bed. My mind felt extremely tired and I couldn't stay awake long enough to read the pages. I had a terrifying dream about Red. In my dream, I was walking through the woods at night when I stumbled across what looked like an unmarked grave. As I looked closely at the grave site, I noticed a foot sticking out of it. As I knelt down, I grabbed some sticks beside me.

Using the sticks in my hands, I started digging through the dirt on the grave. Continuing to dig, I eventually uncovered a body of a boy. As I sat on my knees staring at his body covered in blood, I became eerie of how he died. There was a remarkable amount of blood that made it difficult to determine who the boy was from behind so I decided to roll him over to get a better view of his face. As my heart beat fast, I slowly turned the bloody body over. To my surprise, it was the body of Red. I screamed as I scurried through the woods quickly, then I woke up. I gasped while sweat dripped down my face. Mae jumped up out of bed.

"What is wrong with you Pepper?" Mae asked.

"I had a bad dream." I replied while trying to catch my breath.

"You really scared me. I thought someone was attacking you by the way you screamed." She stated.

"Sorry." I said.

"What was you dreaming about anyway?" She asked.

111

"I found my brother, dead." I replied as I began to cry.

"Ohh." She said softly. *"It was just a dream Pepper. It wasn't real."*

"It was real to me." I stated.

"You will be fine now. The dream is over. Try to go back to sleep before you wake everyone else up." She said.

I turned the opposite direction of Mae to try to go back to sleep. It was difficult not to think about the bad dream I had about Red.

"What did it mean?" I became confused and terrified to sleep. Soon, I saw the sun slowly rising through the window that was on the other side of the room. After awhile, Miss Drake entered the room to get everyone for breakfast. During breakfast, I gazed at my food with no motivation to eat. My mind was in deep thought about what the afterlife would be like. I remembered a moment at Isabelle's funeral. People were gathered around her casket chattering when I overheard someone make a statement; *"She is in a better place now. A place of no pain or hurt. She will not have to suffer anymore." "Could there be such a place?"* I thought

to myself.

Not touching a bite of my breakfast, my mind wandered. By the time lunch came around, I felt genuinely hungry. Wishing I could get another chance to sit with Red to eat, I knew that day would never come again. The reason for the bad dream might have had something to do with the stolen copy pages. Maybe Red didn't want me to read what he wrote, but I was determined to read them anyway and I felt I needed answers in my life. I had to find a quiet place to read them, where no one would see me.

"How are you feeling Pepper?" asked Miss Drake.

"I'm okay." I replied.

*"You don't look okay." S*he stated.

"I have a lot on my mind." I said.

"I know you do. If you need to talk, I am here for you." She replied.

"I know. I will be fine." I said.

"Well, it's time to go study now." Miss Drake stated.

I returned to my room for study time. Later that night, I found it difficult to isolate myself to read Red's pages so I finally gave up and went to bed. I had no problem falling to sleep, and I didn't have any bad dreams like the night before.

Chapter 8

The next day, I was even more determined to find a way to read the pages. I put them back into my pants. While everyone else participated in the school day, I sat in the bathroom alone. This would be the only way I could find out what Red had written. No more interruptions and no more wandering. The time had finally come, I will find out what I have set out to seek. I pulled out the pages and slowly opened them. I read them aloud in a whispering voice.

"My secrets,"

"I went to the basement again after Dad left for work. I am getting closer to finding out what he has been up to. I found a few containers of a type of powdered substance. A couple of the containers were empty with powdered residue in the bottom of them. I read the label, but I didn't recognize the name of the powdered substance. I wrote the name on my hand. I am going to do some research to find out what this powder is. Maybe it will tell me what my dad is up to. Until next time...."

I always wanted to know what Frank was up to in the

basement. He spent a great amount of time down there when Isabelle was sick. At the time, I concluded it was his way to get alone time to grieve over Isabelle's sickness. She had many severe sick moments that were hard for all of us to grasp. No one knew how to help her, so we all grieved. I continued to another page of the book.

"My Secrets,"

"I have done a little research on the powdered substance. It took me some time to figure out what it was. I have learned it's a type of poison. It is not for human consumption. I wander why my dad would have these in a locked basement? This may be why he didn't want Pepper and I to play down there. He was afraid we would get a hold of it. That still doesn't tell me why he has them. What could he be using poison for? Until next time..."

Now I was getting intensely confused. There had to be a good reason Frank would be keeping poison in the basement. Maybe he was doing some kind of experiment for work. He worked in the construction business. I couldn't think of anything they would use poison for in that type of work. Then again, I am no expert.

By the time I finished reading the second copy page, Miss Drake was searching for me. She entered the restroom calling my name. I quickly hid the pages back into my pants to run out.

"Where have you been?" asked Miss Drake.

"I wasn't feeling well so I thought I would sit in here." I replied.

"You have been in this bathroom the whole time?" She asked.

"Yes." I quickly replied.

"Well, if you're not feeling well go to your room. The other girls are going to be in there soon for quiet time." Miss Drake stated.

"Yes ma'am." I said.

I returned quietly to my room. On the way, my mind pertained deep thoughts about what I had read. Up to this point in my life, I tried to make sense of everything that happened. To have a better understanding, I needed to read more of the diary pages.

If I had gotten the chance to look through Frank's file,
I was certain it would contain interesting information about
his past. Until I found out the truth about him, I had no
desire to give up.

After entering my room, I continued to read what Red
had wrote. I knew I had to hurry before the other girls
returned. If I were caught with parts of Red's book, I
wouldn't be able to explain why I had it, so I read as fast as I
could without missing any important information about
Frank. I wanted to know the connection between the poison
and Isabelle's sickness. The worst came to my thoughts.

"My Secrets,"

*I researched more on the poison. I found out it can be
deadly to humans if consumed over a long period of time.
Some of the side effects, if ingested, are severe vomiting,
weakness, stomach pain, migraine headaches, seizure, and
even possible organ failure. There were many other side
effects, too many to mention, but these specific side effects
caught my eye right away. When I came across them, I*

realized these were similar symptoms my mom had when she
was severely sick. Was there a connection between the
poison and Mom's illness? Until next time......"

My mind was totally thoughtless for a moment. I was in disbelief of what I just read. The assumption that Frank poisoned Isabella hit me like a bombshell.

"Could this be true?" The suspense was unbearable so I had to keep reading. The strangeness of what really happened was eating me alive to the point that I wanted to know if Frank really did poison Isabelle. I felt like running away again to go confront Frank about what I know. He couldn't get to me anyway due to being behind bars. I could say what I wanted to him, and he can't do anything about it. He will have to listen to me. I felt no fear about confronting him with the death of Isabelle. As I continued to read, anger built up inside me.

"My Secrets",

"I have proof that my dad poisoned my mom. There is too much of a connection for my dad to deny it. Why would he want to kill her? She was so beautiful and kind hearted. She

didn't deserve to die. I will get my revenge with him. When he least expects it. For now, I have to keep what I know a secret. Until next time...."

Tears ran down my face as I heard the other girls coming. I quickly hid the pages again while wiping my eyes. Mae noticed that I had been crying.

"What is wrong Pepper?" Mae asked.

"Nothing." I replied sadly.

"Don't say nothing. You have been crying." She said.

"I will be fine. I don't want to talk about it." I stated.

"I am your friend. You know I am here for you." said Mae.

"Yes, but I don't feel like talking right now Mae." I replied.

"Fine. When you are ready to talk let me know." She stated as she walked away.

I couldn't get out of bed; I had fallen weak and wasn't sure if I should tell anyone about my discovery. If what Red wrote were true, then Frank was a murderer. The police had this evidence on file. That meant, Frank was going to prison for a long time. He might as well be dead to me too.

The first few weeks of the trial were the most difficult on me and I fell experienced a deep depression like never before. I became terrified someone would to find out what I knew. First it was Frank's secret, then it was Red's secret, and now it is my secret. Suddenly, I could feel the torment and suffering that Red felt inside when he found out what Frank did to Isabelle. Many questions I've been seeking for a long time have finally been answered.

"Why would Frank be so evil?" At this point, I had discovered that answers came with more questions. A few more days of debating whether or not I should confront the officer with the information I knew went through my mind. At lunch Mae decided to strike up another conversation with me. The last time we spoke was when she caught me crying.

"How are you?" Mae asked.

"I have a secret." I replied.

"What kind of secret?" She asked.

"I don't know if I should tell anyone." I said.

"You can tell me. I won't tell anyone anything you say."
She stated.

"Maybe later." I said.

"Okay." She replied.

We finished our lunch to go outside. I paced around
slowly in profound thought about my secret. Mae approached
me about it once again.

*"You have me curious about this secret you are
keeping."* Mae stated.

"I don't know if I am ready to tell anyone yet Mae." I
stated.

*"The longer you keep the secret, the longer it's going
to take you to get better."* She said.

"I know. I am just confused." I said.

"Talk to me Pepper. I am your friend." Mae replied.

"Remember when I went to the police station?" I asked.

"Yes." She replied.

"While I was there, I stole copies of pages from my brother's book out of a file cabinet." I explained.

"You did what?" She asked curiously. *"Don't you know it's against the law to steal?"*

"Yes! I didn't mean to steal, I just seen them when I was looking through his folder. I didn't have time to read them because the officer came into the room, so I threw them in my pants." I said.

"Why would you want your brother's diary?" asked Mae.

"I started reading some of it before his disappearance. I wanted to read more to see if what he wrote could answer some of my questions." I replied.

"What questions?" She asked.

"Questions about why my brother was acting strange before he disappeared." I replied.

"Well, did it answer anything? What did his diary say?" She asked.

"I found out my dad killed my mom. Red wrote about it in his book." I replied.

"I feel angry inside." I stated.

"I could imagine. After everything you have already been through, you find this out." Mae said.

"You know, I think my dad found out that Red knew." I said. *"I heard them argue a few nights before Red went missing. Red wouldn't tell me what it was about though. They could have been arguing over my mom's death. Maybe Red confronted my dad about what he did to her."*

"Could they have been arguing about anything else? What did you hear?" Mae asked.

"I didn't hear anything. But it's all starting to make sense now. And the night Red came up missing, I spilled the beans on him." I replied.

"What do you mean you spilled the beans on him?" She asked.

"I was sneaking into his room to read more of his diary when I was caught by my dad. He wanted to know why I was

out of bed. I got scared and just started telling him everything."
I replied.

"*What's everything Pepper?*" Mae asked.

"*Oh gosh. All this is my fault, Mae.*" I replied
frantically.

"*Calm down. None of this is your fault, Pepper. Tell me
what you said to your dad that night.*" She stated.

"*I told him how Red was acting strange, and that he
was taking me away to protect me.*" I replied.

"*What did he say after you told him that?*" Mae asked.

"*He told me to go back to bed, that he would take care
of it.*" I replied.

"*And Red never came back.*" Mae softly stated.

"*No. see all my fault.*" I cried. "*If I hadn't told my dad
anything, Red would still be alive. He probably went looking
for him and killed him to keep him quiet. He didn't know Red
wrote everything in his diary.*"

"*No Pepper. It's not your fault. Your dad has issues that*

are beyond your control." She replied.

"Red told me not to tell him anything. I should have listened." I continued to cry.

"It's okay. Just take a deep breath and relax before Miss Drake see's you crying. Then you will have to tell everyone about it." Mae said as she tried to comfort me.

"I don't understand life." I said.

"I don't think anyone does." Mae stated.

"Do you believe there is no pain in the afterlife Mae?" I asked.

"Yes, I do Pepper, but I don't want you to do anything dumb." She replied.

"Dumb?" I asked.

"Pepper, I know you are hurting, but you have a whole life to live. Frank has already taken your family. Don't let him take you too." She replied.

"I guess I didn't think of it that way." I said.

"You see Pepper, he is the one suffering in the end. He's

126

the one that will have to sit in prison and think about what he did. He will never get his freedom back. He will never be able to hurt anyone again." She explained.

"Yes, I agree." I said.

"I want you to live happy with your grandma. This is a chance for you to get yourself together. A chance at a new life Pepper." She said.

"Do you think my mom can see me, Mae?" I asked.

I don't really know Pepper. But if she is, she is looking at you proudly for being so brave." She replied.

"I don't feel brave Mae. I have cried." I stated.

"Everyone cries Pepper. It's not a bad thing to cry. That's part of the healing process." Mae said.

"Did you cry when you came here?" I asked.

"Yes. There were many nights I cried. I didn't have a friend to talk to either." She replied.

"If I were here back then, I would have talked to you." I stated.

"I know Pepper. We are great friends together. Don't forget to come back to visit." She replied.

"I will never forget you, Mae." I said.

"I know you won't" She replied.

A few days before the trial was set to end, I received another visit from the officer. He showed up to tell me I was approved to go live with my grandma. I questioned him about the trial, but he refused provide much information. He appeared strikingly confident that Frank would be put away for the rest of his life. I explained to him how furious I felt about everything. He assured me I would never have to deal with Frank again.

I wanted one last visit with Frank after the trial. The officer tried to convince me that it would be more beneficial to let things go. He finally agreed to let me have one after I was persistent about it. I wasn't sure what I would say to him yet, but it wasn't going to be anything nice. Frank had to know exactly how I felt about him destroying my life. I knew this would help me find the peace I needed to move on.

Chapter 9

The trial ended in a double guilty verdict against Frank for the murders of Isabelle and Red. To my surprise, the police had decided to convict him of both murders. He was sentenced to life in prison with no chance of parole. They surely had enough evidence they had to prove his guilt. I still had difficulty understanding his motive for wanting to take the life of Isabelle. She suffered a slow miserable death for no reason.

On the day I decided to visit Frank in prison, the press surrounded the front entrance. They were somehow tipped off about my visitation with him. I didn't feel nervous this time. The anger I had toward Frank was immense. As I marched into the prison, the press were shouting out questions trying to get me to speak. I became too angry to speak to anyone. The only thing I was worried about was seeing Frank. I wanted to know why he took away the people I loved the most.

After finally entering into the prison, I was taken to where Frank was waiting. He was behind a big window of glass. I had to talk to him through a phone.

"Hi Pepper." Frank said sadly.

"Why did you do it?" I asked curiously.

"Do what?" He quickly asked back.

"Stop! Just tell me why you poisoned my mommy!" I yelled angrily.

"How do you know about that?" He asked.

"Don't worry about it. I want to know why." I replied.

"Pepper, I loved your mother dearly. I didn't want to hurt her." He stated.

"You killed her! Then you killed Red! You took away my life..." I said angrily as I began to cry.

"I am sick Pepper!" Frank exclaimed.

"Why didn't you get help?" I asked.

"I thought I could control it. I did good until your mother asked for a divorce. Don't you see pepper, she was having an affair. She didn't love me no more. I couldn't let that happen!" Frank pleaded.

"With who?" I asked.

"It doesn't matter anymore." He replied as he shook his head.

"What about Red?" I asked.

"He didn't understand Pepper. He confronted me about poisoning his mom. I tried to explain to him what had happened. He wasn't hearing it. He threatened to turn me in and take you away." He explained.

"He was trying to protect me from you!" I said angrily.

"I didn't want to hurt anyone. You have to believe me Pepper." Frank stated.

"You should have gotten help. You are dead to me now. I am going to live with my grandma, you know the one I don't know." I said softly.

"Don't do that please. Don't listen to her lies." Frank begged.

"The only person who lives to lie, is you." I stated as I hung the phone up.

I walked out of that prison feeling no better than the minute I walked in. The excuses Frank used to hurt my family, was completely devastating. At this point, I felt no love for him anymore. If Isabelle were having an affair, I would have known it. My parents never fought so I assumed it was another one of Frank's lies to get out of trouble. I refused to believe a word Frank spoke anymore and was ready to leave the facility and move on.

The day came I had to say goodbye to Mae. She comforted me with a lot of advice while I was at the facility.

"So, you finally get to leave." Mae stated.

"Yeah." I said.

"We will all miss you, Pepper." Mae said sadly.

"I will miss all of you too Mae." I replied.

"I wish you the best. I know you will make a good life for yourself." Mae said.

"Thank you for being there for me Mae when I needed you to." I stated.

"Your welcome Pepper. I will never forget you." She

replied.

"Same here." I said.

"You know I am only a phone call away Pepper. If you ever need anything, don't hesitate to contact me." She said.

"I won't Mae. Bye." I said.

"Bye." Mae said as she hugged me.

The first day I left to live with my grandma, she took me out to lunch. All of the publicity was overwhelming. Every time I turned around, I either heard others having conversation about Frank's trial or saw it on the front page of the newspapers that others were reading. The way perceived it; Frank's double murder was the biggest story around since the death of Cherry. We settled at a nice small restaurant hoping to be able to eat a quiet lunch. As we waited on our food, everyone kept staring at us and whispering. A worker approached me.

"Hey, aren't you the little girl that went to the prison?" *A* woman asked.

"Yes." I replied.

"Yeah, I thought so. I see you on television." She said.

"We would like to eat in privacy if you don't mind." My grandma interrupted.

"Yeah, sure." The woman said.

"Thank you." My grandma said back.

As we ate, I sat in silence. People outside the restaurant window were trying to get photos of us.

"Are you okay?" asked Grandma.

"Yes." I replied.

"Don't worry Pepper. We will be out of this city soon." She said.

"Okay." I said.

We finally finished our lunch, then left the city. It made me happy to get away from the stress of Frank's actions. After a few hours, we arrived at my grandma's house. It seemed to be a long drive with short conversation exchanged between us. I assumed Grandma knew I wasn't up to talking much.

It started to get dark when we arrived at Grandma's

house, so I remained inside for the night. I slept in Frank's old room he had growing up. Grandma said she hadn't touched a thing since Frank were last there. I was shocked she actually let me sleep in the room. Grandma claimed she was ready to move on now that she had found her son. Since I knew about Isabelle and Red now, I guess I felt the same way. We would both move on together.

That night appeared strange to me. Grandma was so quiet, it felt like I was alone in a big house. Then the door creaked open.

"Do you need anything before I go to bed?" asked Grandma.

"No." I replied.

"If you are feeling up to it, we can take a walk-through town tomorrow." Grandma said.

"Are there any kids around here?" I asked.

"There are a few. I am sure you will meet some of them." She replied.

"Okay." I said.

"Pepper, I am glad you decided to come stay with me. It gets lonely here by myself. Grandpa would have loved you." She stated.

"What happened to Grandpa?" I asked curiously.

"He died of old age. He talked every night about how much he missed your father. We can look at some pictures tomorrow." Grandma replied.

"Okay." I said again.

"Good night, Pepper." *"Good night, Grandma."* We both exchanged.

I fell asleep quickly, but was soon awakened from a loud thump in my room. At first, I thought someone was trying to break in the house. I slowly raised my head to observe. The room was dark, so I couldn't see much. It was too frightening to get out of bed to turn the lights on, so I snuggled under my blanket tightly hoping not to hear anything else. Then all of a sudden, I heard footsteps. They were coming from above me. The best explanation I could come up with was that Grandma couldn't sleep so she was up walking around. I eventually fell back to sleep.

The next morning, I arose to glance around. Nothing was noticeably out of place. The smell of something good cooking, caught my attention as I jumped out of bed to hurry to the kitchen.

"Good morning. I hope you're hungry. I made some good homemade biscuits and gravy." Grandma said.

"It smells just like mommy use to make it." I said back.

"Well, let's dig in." Grandma said as she smiled.

As we ate, I concluded that the food was the best cooking I had tasted since Isabelle died. I felt extremely comfortable at that moment. It brought back many happy memories for me. After breakfast, Grandma and I scavenged through pictures. I saw pictures of grandpa with Frank. I also saw pictures of Frank in his baby days.

"Grandma, why is daddy the way he is?" I asked.

"I don't know. We tried to give him the best life possible." Grandma replied.

"It looks like he had a very good life here." I said.

"Yes, I thought so. I just can't help to think I could have

done something more to help

him." She said sadly.

"*I am sure you tried your best.*" I stated trying to cheer her up.

"*Maybe. Did you know your father use to be a good piano player?*" Grandma asked.

"*Really. I love playing the piano.*" I replied.

"*You must have picked up your father's talent then.*" She said.

"*Do you have a piano?*" I asked.

"*I sure do. Come on I will show you.*" She said as she walked out of the room.

She escorted me into another room of the house. The piano was covered with a big sheet. As I glanced around the room, I noticed other things were covered also.

"*Why is everything covered up?*" I asked.

"*After your grandpa died, I figured it wouldn't be long before I went too. I started boxing things up and covering things. I am getting too old to keep things clean anymore. I was ready to give up in life. The night I seen Frank's picture on television, a spark of life went through me. I knew it wasn't my time to go yet."* She explained.

"I bet you will live another hundred years Grandma." I replied.

"I wish child." She chuckled.

"May I play with the piano?" I asked.

"Yes. You can play anytime you want." She replied.

I played music on the piano while Grandma listened. She relaxed in a rocking chair in the corner of the room. I continued playing several more songs for grandma before having lunch. We gossiped while we ate.

"You play as good as your father played." Grandma stated.

"I have never heard daddy play. He kept to himself a lot." I said.

"Were you taking lessons?" She asked.

"No. I learned to play on my own." I replied.

"You are a very talented young lady, Pepper." Grandma claimed.

"Thank you." I replied with pride.

"You're welcome." Grandma said with a smile.

"Did you have trouble sleeping last night?" I asked.

"No. I slept very well." Grandma replied.

"Does someone else live here?" I asked.

"No Pepper. Just me and you." She explained.

"But I heard someone walking around in your room above me." I said.

"The only thing above you is the attic. You probably heard an animal. I will have someone come check it out today." She stated.

"Okay. Do you mind if I explore through the house sometime?" I asked.

"I don't mind child. Just be careful not to break

anything. I have a lot of old things around here." Grandma replied.

"Okay. I will be careful." I said.

Grandma's house was big with a bunch of rooms. I was unsure where to start exploring. I decided to start in the attic, where I heard the footsteps. I opened the attic door and stepped slowly up the dark stairs. Suddenly, I heard movement at the top of the stairs. My heart began to pound through my chest. I became so terrified; I hurried out of the attic slamming the door shut.

After that experience, I came to the conclusion that the attic wasn't going to be the first place I explored. Instead, I started with my own room. Frank surely had to have some hidden secrets in there from his younger days. As I was searching through his drawers, I came across a drawer full of different items he had apparently collected. Some were newspaper clippings of several different women that were missing. These clippings dated back as when he was a teenager. There were other items such as watches, necklaces, and rings.

My mind wandered why Frank would want to collect

jewelry. It could have been from an old girlfriend of his he had right before he left town. I wanted to learn who the missing women were. As I read the newspaper clippings that Frank had collected, I noticed a necklace around one of the girl's necks. She wore it in her picture. I looked over to Frank's collection and saw he had the same type of necklace. At that moment, grandma hollered my name. I threw everything back into the drawer and hurried downstairs.

"Yes grandma." I said quickly.

"Did you still want to go into town today?" Grandma asked.

"No. I changed my mind. I will go another day." I replied.

"Are you okay?" She asked.

"Yes. I am not feeling up to going out yet." I replied.

"Have you found anything interesting yet?" She asked.

"No. not really." I replied.

"Well, let me know if you need anything." Grandma said.

"Okay." I said.

Uncertain if grandma had any idea about Frank's collection, I ran back upstairs. I wasn't sure what to do. The collection had to be linked to the women in the newspaper clippings. I began to think Frank somehow had to have something to do with the disappearance of these women. For the rest of the day, I could not explore grandma's house. I was horrified of what else I might discover about Frank. It was probably best to leave the unknown alone.

Grandma came upstairs to get me at dinner time. I proceeded down quietly to eat.

"You know, I was thinking. Maybe I should clean that room out. That way you can make it your own." Grandma said.

"No! I mean-- it's fine grandma." I hesitantly said.

"I figured you would be happy with that." Grandma stated.

"I don't want to make it my own right now. I just want to leave everything alone." I said.

*"Why?" S*he asked.

"I am just not ready for that right now." I replied.

"Okay. Are you sure you're alright?" Grandma asked.

"Yes. I just want to eat and lay down." I replied.

We continued to eat our dinner. Before I left the kitchen, I had one more thing on my mind to question Grandma about.

"What kind of things was daddy into when he was younger?" I asked.

"I am not sure Pepper. He was gone a lot during his teenage years. I couldn't keep up with everything he was out doing." Grandma replied.

"Did he ever talk to you about anything?" I asked.

*"No. I would ask him about what he did, but he would get angry if I asked." S*he replied.

"Oh." I said confused.

"Why do you ask?" Grandma asked.

"I was just curious what he liked to do. I am going to

bed." I replied as I ran back upstairs.

"Good night." Grandma said softly.

Resting in bed engrossed about Frank's collection, I debated half the night as to whether I should tell Grandma and the police about my findings. Frank was already in prison for the rest of his life. I wasn't sure what else they could do to him. At the least, I figured the information could bring closure to the missing girl's family.

The light stayed on in my room for the night. With the walking sounds above me throughout the night, my interest arose about what could be in the attic. The idea frightened me that I would find more secrets from Frank's dark side. I was beginning to think I wasn't going to be able to move on with my life being here with Grandma. Every time I turned around; I was getting slapped with Frank in the face. I was ready to forget about the bad person he was, but I knew that wasn't going to happen anytime soon. Eventually, I exhausted my mind to the point of falling asleep.

Chapter 10

The next day, I took journey through town with Grandma. Summer time had finally come and very warm outside. Grandma lived in a small town a few hours East from the big city I came from. As we strolled through town, I observed some differences from where I previously lived. In the big city, many people dressed in suits for their jobs at big companies. No one in this town dressed in a suit.

"Grandma, where is everyone's suit?" I asked.

"Suit?" She quickly asked back.

"Yes. Back in the city almost everyone wore a suit for their jobs." I replied.

"The only time you will see someone wearing a suit in this town is on Sunday morning child." Grandma said.

"What's so special about Sunday morning?" I asked.

"Church Pepper. Have you ever been to church?" She asked.

"No." I replied.

"Well, you will go to church living here. Everyone in town gathers for church once a week." Grandma said.

"Even kids?" I asked.

"Yes. Even kids Pepper." She said.

We stopped in a clothing store to look around. The streets were full of old antique and clothing stores connected to each other. Grandma got busy talking to a woman about purses, so I ambled to the other side of the store glancing through clothes.

"May I help you find something today young lady?" A woman said.

"No. I am just here with my grandma." I replied.

"Oh, so you are the famous new kid in town." She stated sarcastically.

"Famous?" I asked.

"Yeah, your Frank's daughter, right?" She asked.

"Yes, but--" I started to be confused.

"I thought so. He is an evil man you know." She

interrupted.

"You knew him?" I asked.

"Knew him? I dated him at one time. Seems like it was a good choice getting away from him." She replied.

"Why did you guys break up?" I curiously asked.

"He was a violent man. I thought he was going to kill me a few times." The woman replied.

"Were you ever sick?" I asked a few minutes later.

"Yes. Every time he took me out, I came home sick. So, I told him I wasn't going out with him no more. I told him I didn't want see him no more." She replied.

"What did he say?" I asked.

"He became angry that night. I heard he went home and started a big fight with his father. No one heard from him after that. His mother said he skipped town and she didn't know where he was. I didn't care. I was glad he was gone." She replied.

Grandma came over and we left. We stopped at an ice

cream shop on the way home. As we sat there, I thought a lot about what the woman at the clothing store had told me.

"Do you know that woman I was talking to at the clothing store?" I asked Grandma.

"Yes. Her name is Paula. She is an old girlfriend of your father." Grandma replied.

"Did he like her?" I asked.

"I assumed that he did. He never talked much about the people he hung around." She replied.

"Paula told me she broke up with daddy the night he left town." I stated.

"Well, that would explain why he came home wanting to fight with your grandpa." She said.

"Grandma, I think he was making her sick, just like he made mommy sick." I stated with concern.

"What do you mean?" She asked.

"Paula said every time she went out with daddy, she came home sick. So, she told daddy she wasn't going out with

him anymore." I replied.

"I don't know how true any of that is. Don't go assuming things without proof Pepper" Grandma stated.

"If I showed you proof of something, what would you do?" I asked curiously.

"I don't know. Depends on what it is. What do you have proof of Pepper?" Grandma asked.

"I have something to show you when we get home Grandma." I said.

After finishing our ice cream, we returned home. Grandma followed me upstairs to Frank's old room. She settled quietly on the side of the bed as I opened his collection drawer. I slowly handed the newspaper clippings of the missing women to Grandma.

"What are these?" Grandma asked.

"They are missing women Grandma." I replied.

"Why do you have these?" She asked.

"I found them. Those were some of the things daddy

collected." I replied.

"Well, I am sure he was just curious about what happened to these missing girls Pepper." Grandma assumed.

"Grandma, I think he had something to do with their disappearance." I stated firmly.

"Now why would you say that?" asked Grandma.

"Look. This is the jewelry that belonged to the missing girls." I replied as I slowly handed her the jewelry.

Grandma stared at the jewelry and the newspaper clippings for a few minutes in silence.

"I don't know what to say about this Pepper." Grandma said as she started to cry.

"I'm sorry. I just wanted you to know." I said.

"I guess I should call the sheriff to come out." She said sadly.

She arose from the bed and shuffled slowly out of the room. I left Frank's collection sitting on the side of the bed while I went downstairs to accompany Grandma. We waited on the sheriff to show up. I could see the distress on Grandma's face as she sat at the kitchen table.

"Are you okay Grandma?" I asked.

"I will be fine child. I should have known he was up to no good. I had a feeling something was wrong with him. I tried to talk to him about things. I wanted to help him. He wouldn't let me in. He treated me bad." She replied.

"What did he do to you?" I asked.

"He use to hit me. He has threatened my life several times. That's why your grandpa never got along with him. He didn't like the way your father treated me." She replied sadly.

There was a knock at the door. It was the sheriff. Grandma escorted him upstairs to show him Frank's collection. I was advised to stay downstairs while the sheriff investigated, but I thought it was unfair since I was the one who discovered the items. It wasn't long before other police officers showed up to Grandma's house. They searched through Frank's old room looking for more evidence against him. I patiently waited outside to find out what they were going to discover.

A few hours went by before everyone was finally gone. Grandma came to accompany me on the front porch.

"Did they find anything else?" I asked.

"A few things, but that's not important right now." Grandma replied.

"What's going to happen to Frank?" I asked.

"I don't know." She replied.

"Did they know who the missing women were?" I asked.

"Yes. They have never been able to solve their cases until now. You were brave coming to me about what you found." replied Grandma.

"Will they find the missing women now?" I asked.

"I am sure they will. They will have to talk to your daddy about it. I am sure he will tell them where the girls are. I don't want you to worry about that anymore Pepper." Grandma explained.

After sitting on the porch for awhile, we returned

inside to get dinner. While eating, Grandma wanted to discuss switching rooms.

"I have an extra room upstairs at the end of the hall. After dinner, we can move your things into there." Grandma said.

"Why do I have to switch rooms?" I asked.

"The police don't want anyone in there right now. They may have to come back to collect more things." She replied.

"Okay." I said.

"And, I think it would be best if you didn't explore anymore of the house right now." Grandma continued.

"Why not?" I asked.

"I am not up to anymore discoveries about my son. Just leave it be." She replied.

"Okay Grandma." I said with my head down.

"Let's go get your things moved, so you can go to bed Pepper." Grandma said.

Grandma helped me move my things into another room.

It was a bigger room than I had before. She claimed she used it as a guest bedroom for when company came to stay. Grandma explained that it was my new permanent room now and that I could do whatever I wanted with it. I wasn't allowed to go into Frank's old room anymore, but it didn't bother me. Maybe now I wouldn't hear the footsteps at night.

Grandma tucked me into bed for the night before leaving the room. I wasn't really tired, but I remained in bed anyway. It appeared we were going to get a storm coming through. My bed was next to a window where I could lay in bed while I observed outside. I noticed a big building out back behind grandma's house. I wandered what she used it for.

The doors to the big building were slamming open and shut as the wind picked up from the storm. It was so loud; I was surprised Grandma couldn't hear it. It might have been because her room was in the front of the house. I was moved to a room in the back of the house now. It seemed so far away from Grandma, but really, I was only at the other end of the hallway. The footstep sounds were unheard in the new room. I decided I should try to get some sleep.

The next morning, Grandma called me down for

breakfast.

"I have to go somewhere this morning." Grandma said.

"Where?" I asked.

"I have to go into town for a doctor checkup. You will be fine here for a few hours. I expect you to behave and not wander off while I am gone." She said.

"Yes grandma." I replied.

"You sit here and finish your breakfast. I will be back as soon as I can." said Grandma as she started to walk away.

"Grandma, what is that big building out back?" I asked.

"That's a barn. We use to keep animals in it at one time. After your grandpa passed away, I got rid of them all. There is nothing out there for you. I have to go. I will see you in a bit." Grandma explained.

After Grandma left, I returned back upstairs to rest. I stared at the big barn out back in contemplating. I knew Grandma forbid me to explore anymore, but something was drawing my attention to the barn. Curiosity got the best of me once again and I went out back to check out the barn.

I trampled across the muddy ground to the opening of the barn. It was dark and scary inside. The only light was from the sun shining through a couple side windows. I stepped inside to inspect. I observed a few stalls that animals previously lived in. I glanced down to the other side of the barn and noticed a ladder. I slowly made my way to the ladder and climbed up to a loft area.

The loft was one huge room full of hay. There was, what looked like, an old antique chest over in the corner, so I crawled over to check it out. I stopped in front of the chest to open it. Inside was a map that was folded. As I unfolded the map, I noticed dot marks and areas on the map that were circled. My mind wandered if this could be more of Frank's collection he tried to hide. I assumed Grandma would get furious with me if she found out I was exploring again, so I hesitated to tell her.

I was unsure as to whether the areas that were circled on the map indicated the locations of the missing girls. As I examined closer, I noticed my old city had been dotted, so I became puzzled by what this meant. As I searched through more of the items in the chest, I discovered a few old pictures of Frank and my grandpa. They were pictures from fishing trips they had taken together. Frank didn't appear to be any older than I was now. It seemed as if they were close at one time.

The sounds of a car driving up in Grandma's driveway startled me. I closed the chest and raced back toward the house with the folded map. A man saw me coming around front from the side of the house.

"Where are you coming from?" Asked the man.

"I was playing out back." I replied.

"I can see. Your feet are muddy child. You should take your shoes off before you enter the house. What is your name?" He asked.

"Pepper." I replied.

"You must be the granddaughter I have heard so much about." He proudly stated.

"I guess so. My grandma is at the doctor." I said.

"I know. I am supposed to meet her here afterward for

coffee. " He said.

"We can wait on the porch. I am sure she will be here soon. " I said.

"That sounds like a good idea. " The man said.

I removed my shoes and waited on the porch with Grandma's friend. We spoke shortly as he slowly swung back and forth on Grandma's porch swing. He chatted a little about church so I explained to him that Grandma was going to start taking me on Sunday's. It wasn't long before Grandma had arrived back home. She introduced her friend as George, an acquaintance from church. As they started to step into the house to have coffee, something caught Grandma's eyes.

"What do you have in your hands? " She asked.

"It's-- a map. " I hesitantly replied.

"Wait. Let me see that. " Grandma said as she took the map out of my hands.

Grandma opened the folded map and glared at it for a minute.

"I see you have been exploring again. " Grandma

stated.

"I was playing in the barn and found it." I said.

"You shouldn't play in the barn Pepper. You could get hurt." She said.

"What is it Grandma?" I asked.

"It's a map. It belonged to your grandpa. He used it after your father left town to try to locate your father." Grandma replied.

"What does the circles and dots mean?" I asked.

"Grandpa dotted the places on the map that he was going to search. Each area he circled meant that he couldn't locate your father in that area." She replied.

"My old city has a dot, but it wasn't circled." I said.

"Yes. That was the last area he dotted to search before he died. He never got the chance to search the city for your father." Grandma said.

"Why did he want to search for daddy?" I asked.

"He was doing it for me. He seen how sad I became

after your father left town. We thought he would return once he cooled down, but after a few years we knew he wasn't coming home again." She replied.

"I wander why daddy didn't want us to know you." I stated.

"I don't know. I am thinking it probably had something to do with his issues he had. Maybe he didn't want you all to find out about what he had done in his past." Grandma said.

"That makes sense. He was full of secrets and lies. Do you think he really wanted to change?" I asked.

"Yes. I truly believe he didn't want to be the monster he was." She replied.

Grandma appeared sad, so I didn't want to force her to talk about Frank anymore. I left her alone to have coffee with her friend George. Later, we had dinner and George left for the night. Grandma and I didn't speak much after he left. I eventually told Grandma I was going to bed and trotted upstairs to my room.

Before Grandma turned in for the night, she checked on me. Seeing Grandma sad made me want to do something to cheer her up. It was never meant to cause her unhappiness in any way. I decided to make her a "thank you" card for being nice to me so I found construction paper and markers. After creating her card, I quietly tipped-toed downstairs to put it on the table where Grandma would see it the next morning. Then I went to bed.

I imagined what Frank would have done if my grandpa had lived long enough to find us. Knowing Frank, he might have been hostile. It was difficult to comprehend why he hated his parents so much. They would have helped him through anything. The way Grandma spoke, Frank meant the world to her. I fell to sleep discouraged about the way he lived his life.

Chapter 11

The next morning Grandma discovered the card I made her. She became so delighted that she surprised me with breakfast in bed. It appeared as if everything were back to normal and were going to be okay for us. With school starting back in a few months, I would have the chance to make new friends around town. Life appeared good for the moment.

A few days later, I found myself alone again in Grandma's big house. As I gazed out the window at the beautiful morning sky, a loud thump from above startled me, so I turned quickly to observe my surroundings. I knew it had come from the attic. I grabbed a flashlight and opened the attic door.

"Hello! Is anyone there?" I asked in a shaky voice.

A few seconds went by with no reply. The further I inched up the stairs, the more anxious I became. I shun the flashlight in front of me in fear that something would jump out at me at any moment. As I reached the top of the stairs, I could hear shuffling sounds coming from the corner of the attic. At that moment, I became extremely frightened shivering in my own shoes.

"Who is there?" I asked softly.

Again, there was no answer. While ambling toward the sounds, I saw a dark shadow moving around.

"Hello." I whispered out.

Suddenly, I came to a complete stop and looked ahead of me. After a few minutes, I realized I was staring through the darkness into the eyes of another person. The shadowy figure I had feared, was that of a young girl.

"Why are you up here?" I asked.

"I followed you from the big city." She replied.

"Followed me? So, you have been up here the whole time?" I asked.

"Yes. I didn't mean to scare you." The girl replied.

"Where is your mom?" I curiously asked.

"I don't know. I can't find her." She replied sadly.

"What about your dad?" I asked.

"He didn't want me." She softly replied.

"Well, you can't stay in this attic. Grandma would get mad if she knew you were hiding up here. Come on, I will take you to the barn. No one will find you out there." I stated.

I quickly escorted the girl to the big barn out back of Grandma's house.

"You can stay in the loft for awhile. I will come out to visit you when I can." I said as I pointed up the ladder.

"Will you help me find my mom?" The girl asked.

"I don't know if I can or not. I'm young myself you know. Grandma wouldn't like it if I left town to look for your mom. We can talk about it another time. For now, just stay in the loft out of sight." I replied.

As I watched the girl slowly climb the ladder toward the loft, the sounds of a car approaching caught my attention. I quickly ran back to Grandma's house to try to sneak upstairs, but Grandma saw me.

"Why were you outside?" Grandma asked.

"I was enjoying the fresh air." I quickly replied.

"I saw you running from the barn." She stated.

"You know me and my exploring." I chuckled trying to shrug it off.

"There's nothing in there for young girls like yourself. Try to stay out of there Pepper." said Grandma.

"Yes ma'am." I said as I ran up the stairs.

Over the next few weeks, I visited the barn everyday and became friends with the mysterious girl from the attic and kept her a secret from Grandma. The girl didn't talk about much. She wanted to find her mom, but I didn't know how to help her. The mom was probably back in the city, somewhere I knew I couldn't return. I encouraged the girl to play and have fun so she wasn't so sad.

One day, we found a little bike behind the barn that my grandpa must have owned. The mysterious girl watched while I rode it around the yard. Riding it made me feel free, like I was flying through the wind. My new friend wouldn't get on it. A couple more weeks went by before I could convince my friend to accompany me on walks.

A nice lady lived down the street from Grandma's

house that enjoyed baking cookies. I stopped to chat with her from time to time while out walking with my friend. She prepared everything she made from scratch. When she saw me strolling past her house, she brought out a big pan of fudge to share. The mysterious girl would never eat any.

"Why don't you ever eat?" I asked.

"I never get hungry." She replied.

"Really?" I confusedly asked.

I was always hungry, especially for cookies. One day the lady quite making cookies and I never saw her again. Even though I never knew what happened to her, I always missed her cookies she baked for me. As time went on, I assumed she moved out of town.

An old scary house was not far from where we lived. My friend and I hiked through the woods to where it sat. We always went through it and played outside of it. The oddness of how it was built attracted me. The inside appeared a little scary, but it did not keep me from entering every room. We visited the old house on many other occasions also. One night at dinner, Grandma became curious about my everyday activity.

"*Where do you wander off too so much Pepper?*" Grandma asked.

"*Nowhere far Grandma.*" I replied.

"*Have you made any friends around town yet?*" Grandma asked.

"*I have made one friend. She seems a little strange though. Grandma, I have never seen her eat. She doesn't play much either. She mainly walks around and talks.*" I replied.

"*I am sure she eats. You have to eat to live Pepper.*" Grandma stated.

"*Yeah, I'm sure she eats somehow.*" I replied.

"*Don't worry yourself.*" She said.

"*Could I invite her over for dinner sometime?*" I asked.

"*Well sure you can. We don't get many visitors around here.*" Grandma replied.

In the neighborhood we lived in, there were little houses and people. The mysterious girl was the only friend I really had. I associated with a few girls on Sunday at church, but we never hung out much. To my surprise, I convinced my mysterious friend to play at a small creek with me one day. It had a cement ledge that ran over the creek. We decided to walk across the ledge. The creek was shallow and full of big rocks. It also had a big tunnel that water flowed through to an opening on the other side of the street.

"Would you like to eat dinner at my house tonight?" I asked. *"We can't tell grandma that you are staying in the barn, but you can come eat with us."*

"No. I am fine." The girl replied as we kept balancing on the ledge.

We creeped along the thin ledge like we were in a circus trying to balance on the high ropes above the crowd.

"You know, your strange. How are you alive if you never eat?" I asked.

All of a sudden, my friend lost her balance and grabbed a hold of me, causing me to lose my balance as well. As we fell toward the creek below, Red came out of nowhere and caught me. That was the last thing I remembered before passing out. I woke up and saw Grandma crying over me.

"What was you thinking Pepper?" She asked angrily.

"What do you mean? Where am I?" I asked confusedly.

"You are at the doctor office. When you didn't come home, a few of us around town searched for you. We found you in the creek unconscious." Grandma explained.

"Red caught me before I hit the creek Grandma." I said.

"Pepper, you hit your head pretty hard. It probably caused you to hallucinate." Grandma stated.

"But I really did see Red. I saw his ghost Grandma. He is watching over me." I explained.

"I'm sure he is. You could have been hurt a lot worse. Stay away from that creek Pepper." Grandma said.

"Is my friend, okay?" I asked.

"What friend?" Grandma asked.

"The girl I was with. She fell into the creek with me." I replied.

"Pepper, there was nobody else in the creek. Who was the friend you were with?" Grandma asked.

"I don't know her name. She has been staying in your barn." I replied.

Grandma looked at me puzzled, as if I didn't know what I were saying.

"Take her home to rest. I think she will be just fine now." the doctor said to Grandma.

We returned to grandma's house and she tucked me into bed.

"Now I want you to stay in bed and rest. You need to give that lump on your head time to heal." Grandma stated.

"Okay Grandma." I said.

Confusion overcame my mind about the mysterious girl. I wanted to know who she was and why she really followed me here. It was too dark to go outside, so I would have to wait till morning to get my answers. As I started to fall to sleep, I heard the floors creak from the attic. Suddenly, I arose from my bed in anger and marched up the attic steps to confront the mysterious girl.

"Where are you?" I asked angrily. *"I know you are up here. I heard you. Come out now!"*

As I glanced around the room, everything was silent. You could hear a needle drop it was so quite, but I never heard a sound. After a few minutes, I went around the attic looking behind everything. I knew she was up there somewhere and I was determined to find her. My mind became so hostile, I began throwing things out of my way. The banging sounds awoke Grandma.

"Pepper! What are you doing in the attic?" Grandma asked.

"I know she's up here somewhere!" I yelled.

"Who Pepper?" She asked confused.

"That girl! I heard her! She is up here and I am going to find her!" I exclaimed.

"That's enough! Calm down!" Grandma yelled as she grabbed me.

I stopped and stared at Grandma.

"Pepper, I don't know what is going on, but you have to stop this. There is no one up here." She said.

"But I heard her." I softly said.

"Whatever you heard is not here now. Let's go back to bed and we will talk about it in the morning." Grandma said.

Grandma locked the attic door as we returned to our rooms. She refused to let me go up there anymore. I rested in bed envisioning the outrage I experienced in the attic. I had no desire to become my father in any way. It left me feeling quite disappointed in myself for not being in control for the few minutes I became angry.

I napped in my bed for the next few days. Grandma brought me food when I was hungry. We never discussed my prior rage through the attic. It appeared quiet around the house, as if the mysterious girl had finally left. I expected everything would be normal again from this point on.

Eventually, I came to the point where I was ready to get out of bed. Grandma said the lump on my head looked much better. Weird things began to happen around the house. Grandma decided to take me into town for lunch. While I was upstairs getting ready, I suddenly heard loud thumps coming from the stairs. I quickly ran to see what had happened. Grandma was laying at the bottom of the steps.

"Are you okay?" I asked in a worried voice.

"Yes." Grandma replied as she tried to get up.

"What happened?" I asked as I ran down the stairs to help her.

"I don't know. I must have lost my balance coming down the stairs and fell." Grandma replied confused.

"Here let me help you." I said while helping grandma up off the floor.

I helped Grandma walk over to her chair where she sat down. She appeared to be in a little pain.

"I am going to call the doctor to come check me out. Go in the kitchen and make you a sandwich for lunch." Grandma said while dialing the doctor.

After making a sandwich, I settled at the kitchen table hoping Grandma would be alright from her fall. Soon after, I heard the doctor arrive to check Grandma out. Even though they were purposely being quiet about it, I overheard their conversation from the kitchen.

"How did you fall?" Asked the doctor.

"I don't know. It was almost like someone pushed me down the stairs." Grandma

replied.

"Pushed you?" He asked.

"Yes. I could feel little hands on me, but when I looked nothing was there." She replied.

"Are you sure it wasn't Pepper?" The doctor asked.

"Pepper? No sir. She was in her room. And I don't want a word of this getting out. Pepper has been through enough lately." Grandma replied.

"I won't say anything, but you probably just lost your balance then." He said.

"Yeah, probably." She said back.

After listening to their conversation back and forth, I became even more confused. I considered if it could be possible that something did push Grandma down the stairs, or even if it were a coincidence that I got pulled off the ledge at the creek. Somehow, I sensed the mysterious girl I met in the attic had something to do with Grandma's fall.

Quietly, I inched out the back door in the kitchen while the doctor was keeping Grandma occupied. I needed to look in the barn for the girl to get answers. After entering the barn, I felt a cool breeze move around me. Suddenly, I broke out with chills all over my body. It seemed to be odd since it was still summer time. Continuing my way to the loft, the mysterious girl was not in sight anywhere, so I decided to go back into the house to check on Grandma.

As I was leaving the barn, I heard a voice speak to me; *"You should leave this place Pepper. There's evil here."*

I quickly turned around, but no one was there.

"Where are you? What do you want?" I asked.

There was no reply. I ran back into Grandma's house and slammed the door shut. The doctor stepped into the kitchen.

"Are you okay in here?" Asked the doctor.

"Yes." I replied.

"What is wrong child?" The doctor asked. *"You look like you have just seen a ghost."*

"Ghost? Why would you say that?" I asked quickly.

"It's a figure of speech Pepper. You look terrified." He replied.

"I'm fine. There's nothing wrong." I said as I ran out of the kitchen.

"Grandma, I don't feel well. I'm going to my room for a while." I said.

"Is something wrong?" Grandma asked.

"No." I replied quickly as I ran upstairs.

A few days passed with no incidents. I began to believe the voice I heard was due to the concussion I had. Grandma was feeling better from her fall down the stairs. She made a big dinner for us to eat.

"What's the big dinner for?" I asked.

"I just thought it be nice for a change." Grandma

replied.

"It sure does look good." I said with a smile.

"Let's eat and find out." Grandma happily said back.

We chatted while we ate dinner. It felt nice for everything to be normal. About halfway through dinner, the lights started flickering on and off. I looked at Grandma in fear.

"Everything will be okay Pepper. It's probably bad electricity. This house is old and could use some updates." Grandma said trying to make me feel better.

The lights finally stopped flickering out. I helped Grandma put the leftover food away. We had just cleaned up from dinner when we heard a loud crashing noise come from the living room. We both scurried to see what it was. All of Grandma's pictures had fallen off the wall. We were standing in the doorway in disbelief. Every picture was shattered all over the floor. Grandma knelt in tears as she started to clean the mess up. I knelt down beside her to help. Not a word was spoke between us the whole time.

After cleaning the big mess up in the living room, we

called it a night. We said our good nights to each other and went to bed. My mind didn't know what to think about the things that happened this evening. I was not only scared, but had no answers for any of it. As I drifted off to sleep, I hoped we would have better days to come.

Chapter 12

The end of summer was approaching and things hadn't settled down around the house. Actually, it had gotten worse. I chose to go into town with Grandma to help her get a few groceries. It felt nice to get out after spending the last few weeks in the house.

"It's a warm day out." I happily stated.

"Yes, it is." Grandma replied.

"Grandma, why do you think bad things are happening around the house?" I asked.

"The falls are probably due to my balance. I'm not young anymore. And I probably didn't hang them pictures through the house very well, or the nails are just old and flimsy now." She replied.

"Do you believe in ghosts?" I asked.

"I can't say that I don't, but I have never seen any." She replied.

"Do you think ghosts can harm people?" I asked.

"*What are all these questions about?*" Grandma quickly asked back.

"*I just wander about things sometimes.*" I replied.

"*No need to wander Pepper. Enjoy life while you can.*" She said.

While shopping in one of the local stores, Grandma suddenly fell sick. As she turned to me to speak, she feels lifeless to the floor. Everyone in the store surrounded her in a matter of minutes. I wasn't sure what to do so I ran to get the doctor.

I didn't stop running until I reached the doctor's office. I stormed into his small building.

"*Grandma needs you now!*" I yelled.

"*Whoa... slow down. What is wrong?*" The doctor asked.

"*We were grocery shopping and Grandma passed out. She is at the store and--*" I tried to explain without breath.

"*Let's go, hurry.*" He interrupted.

The doctor drove me back to the store in his car, where he then told me to stay in the put while he helped Grandma. While waiting, I grew extremely anxious if Grandma would be fine. A few more long minutes went by before the doctor came out. He was slowly escorting Grandma to his car. What a relief I felt watching Grandma limp out of that store.

"Are you okay Grandma?" I asked.

"She doesn't need to speak right now." The doctor quickly replied.

"Are you taking her to a hospital?" I asked.

"No. I am taking her home." He replied.

"But, don't you think she needs to go to the hospital?" I asked.

"We don't go to hospitals around here much. We let life take its course." He replied.

"What does that mean?" I asked.

"Pepper, you will understand someday. But for now, just let me take care of things." The doctor replied.

After returning home, the doctor helped Grandma upstairs to her bed. He stayed awhile to make sure she was fine. Later that evening, a few of Grandma's friends from the church stopped by. They decided to stay a few days to help take care of Grandma. As I rested on the porch, the doctor came out to leave.

"Is Grandma okay?" I asked.

"She is for now." The doctor replied.

"Is something wrong with her?" I curiously asked.

"She's getting old Pepper." He replied.

"Is she going to die?" I curiously asked.

"I am afraid sooner than later." He replied.

"How can I help her?" I asked.

"You can't. Just let her be." He replied.

"We can't do anything?" I asked.

"She's lived a long healthy life. She is tired now. Let her rest." He stated.

No matter what the doctor said, I still believed there was something we could do to help Grandma. It felt he didn't want to help her much. I sat by Grandma's side for a few minutes each night before going to bed. One night as I sat by her, I heard the floors creak in her room. It was as if someone had walked up beside the bed. I quickly turned my head to look. There stood the mysterious girl.

"What are you doing here?" I asked angrily.

"It's time for your Grandma to go soon." The girl replied.

"What are you talking about? How did you get in here?" I asked.

"Your grandma is going to be with her husband. He is waiting for her patiently." She replied quietly.

"You are a ghost?" I confusedly asked.

"Yes." She replied.

"Why are you following me?" I asked.

"You took my necklace. That was the only thing my mother left for me after she

abandoned me and gave me to my father. I waited by my grave everyday for her to return. The necklace was there for her to be able to find me. She would have to remember the necklace. When you took it, I had nothing there for her to see." The mysterious girl replied.

"Cherry... The little girl who was killed by her drunk father. I thought it was something that someone dropped. I didn't mean to take your necklace." I said.

"I can't go back until you return the necklace to my grave." She said.

"Leave me alone! You are just my imagination!" I screamed loudly.

My Grandma's friends suddenly come running into the room as I ran out. I slammed my door shut and jumped on my bed trying to understand why I could see ghosts. They appeared very real at first. Everyone around me was probably a ghost. I believed the whole town might not be real. Maybe I was imagining everything around me. My thoughts and experiences were the reasons for my frustrations. I didn't want to deal with life anymore, so I rested in my bed for the remainder of the day.

About a week went by before Grandma passed on. Being curious, I was not sure where I was going to go now. After the funeral, the towns people returned to Grandma's house to gather in remembrance. The church people cared for me over the next few weeks at their houses. I didn't speak or play with the kids much. One night, I overheard a conversation between a couple I was staying with.

"I don't think she's happy here." Stated the woman.

"What should we do?" Asked the man.

"I don't know. Maybe I can try to get a hold of some of her family. She has to have someone out there somewhere." She replied.

"What if we can't find anyone?" He asked.

"We have to find someone. I will start searching in the morning." She relied.

A few moments later, I proceeded to bed like I never heard anything. Truthfully, I wasn't happy there, but I knew they weren't going to find any of my family. I didn't feel like anyone wanted me. In time, I fell asleep reflecting on how much I would miss Grandma.

After about a month, I took a walk around alone. I found my way back to Grandma's house where I found her church friend George.

"How are you, Pepper?" George asked.

"I'm fine I guess." I replied.

"Did you know the city cops are on their way here?" He asked.

"No. Why?" I asked confused.

"To pick you up." George replied.

"No! I won't go back to that facility again!" I yelled as I jumped up to run.

"Pepper stops!" He yelled as I ran away.

In fear, I ran to the barn behind Grandma's house to hide. I refused to return to the facility to live, so I would find my own place to go. Hunkering myself in the loft, I peeked out the big window. Awhile later, I caught sight of George marching into the barn.

"Pepper, I know you are in here. Come out so I can talk

to you." George hollered.

"No! I'm not going back there." I angrily replied.

"No one said you had to go back there." He said.

"You said the city cops were on their way. That's where they will take me." I said back.

"Well, yes I said they were on their way, but you didn't let me finish before you scattered away from me." said George.

I slowly made my way down the ladder. As I reached the bottom, George approached me.

"What do you want?" I asked.

"Look, the city cops are bringing your aunt with them. There has been some talk about maybe you wanting to go stay with her for awhile." George replied.

"Who said I would want to?" I asked in a smart way.

"It would be better than living at the facility, wouldn't it?" He asked.

"I guess so." I replied.

"I think you will be just fine with your aunt. Now come on." He said.

George walked by my side back to the house. We chatted awhile before George decided to take me back to where I was staying. By the time we returned, the city police had arrived. My aunt Leslie hurried over to comfort me.

"Pepper, I am so sorry about Grandma." Leslie said.

"It's okay." I said.

"Come stay with me. I have plenty of room on the island. It would only be the two of us in the house." Leslie begged.

"Can I bring my things." I asked.

"Of course, you can. We can take it with us to the island." She replied.

I glanced over at George.

"What is going to happen to all of Grandma's things?" I asked.

"Most of it is being sold already to pay for the funeral.

The rest will go to charity." George replied.

"May I keep some pictures of the family?" I asked.

"You can take whatever you want Pepper." He replied.

Later, I was driven back to Grandma's house to pack some of my things, being sure to take some of the pictures Grandma had shown me from her albums. I didn't really want to leave Grandma's house, but I knew I had no choice. Our time was short together, but I grew to like Grandma. Hopefully once I settled on the island, I wouldn't have to move again.

Afraid, I wasn't sure what kind of life to expect on the island. I pondered on it for hours as we traveled to the island. We eventually approached a big boat.

"What are we doing now aunt Leslie?" I asked.

"We are at a ferry." She replied.

"Why?" I curiously asked.

"It's going to take us over to the island." Leslie replied.

"Why can't we drive?" I asked.

"There are no roads that go to the island. The only way on and off is by this ferry boat." She replied.

As the ferry took us to our destination, I admired the nature around me. It was a beautiful day. The sky was a baby blue, and the sun was sparkling bright. I saw a few different islands with lots of trees.

"Beautiful out here, isn't it?" Leslie asked.

"Yes." I replied.

"Your mother loved it out here." She stated.

"Did she visit a lot?" I asked.

"About twice a year, until a year or so before she died." She replied.

"I don't know why daddy would harm her like that." I said sadly.

"Me either. She was crazy about your dad. But I remember the last time she came to visit, she said she asked him for a divorce." Leslie said.

"Why?" I asked.

"She said she didn't love him anymore, that he tried to be controlling over her. "She replied.

"Daddy said she was having an affair. " I said.

"If your mother were having an affair, I sure would have been the first one to know. " Leslie quickly said.

"How can you be so sure? " I asked.

*"Your mother and I told each other everything. Up until she became ill, we talked to each other just about everyday on the phone. " S*he replied.

"Do you think daddy would lie about it? " I asked.

"I wouldn't put anything past Frank. He is pure evil. So, what made you decide to go live with his mother? " Leslie asked.

"I don't know. I wanted to get to know her I guess. " I replied.

"Well, what did you think of her? " She asked.

"I liked her. She was nice. " I replied.

Finally, we arrived on the island. We knew there wasn't

going to be much daylight left, therefore we moved my things to the house quickly. After getting settled in, we ate and went to bed. As I lay staring into the darkness, determination of what my future held wandered my mind. I couldn't help but debate whether or not I had made the right choice to stay with my aunt Leslie. The island appeared to be a safe place, but I had hoped I wouldn't get anymore visitors from the deceased.

After a month of being on the island, school had begun. Life appeared to be good for a change. I made a few friends and helped Leslie around the house after school when I could. We seemed to get along well, and we were both happy. The chance had finally come to feel what a normal life was like again. Making the decision to live with Leslie was the best choice I had made in a long time. I had come to the conclusion that there would be no more ghost visits from this point on.

Leslie's house appeared a little weird. It contained three levels that had a staircase beginning at the top level spiraling down to the bottom level. The upper level was just a big open loft that looked down into the living room. The entrance level had the living and dining room, along with a kitchen. The lower level was built underground. That's where all the bedrooms and bathroom were located. It was a nice house, and a one of a kind.

Leslie cooked just as well as Isabelle did. At this point, I was enjoying life to the fullest. One morning, I was outside helping Leslie plant flowers around her house.

"You seem to be happy here." Leslie stated.

"I miss Grandma, but I like it here." I said.

"Do you like school? Are you making friends?" She asked.

"Yes." I replied.

"Maybe you can have a sleepover sometime. I can make up a lot of snacks." Leslie suggested trying to encourage me.

"That sounds fun. People always ask me why I'm here and not with my family." I said.

"What do you tell them?" She asked.

"I don't know what to say." I replied.

"Well, I am your family. You can say you are visiting for awhile. No one needs to know what happened." She said.

194

"Yeah, I guess so. But I can't keep it a secret forever. What if they eventually find out?" I asked.

"I wouldn't worry about that right now. If they are your friend, then they wouldn't care where you came from." Leslie replied.

We finished planting the flowers around Leslie's house. As I began to walk inside, something strange caught my eye. A woman was out in the front yard next door. She was on the ground in a fetal position. I assumed something were wrong with her.

"Leslie, who is that woman?" I curiously asked.

"That's the neighbor's daughter. She has always lived with her parents." She replied.

"Is something wrong with her?" I asked.

"I don't know much about her. They moved to the island, and keep to their self. They bother no one, and nobody bothers them." Leslie replied.

"So, they never go anywhere?" I asked.

"I have seen the mother a few times getting food and

things they need, but when I tried to speak to her, she kept walking." She replied.

We cleaned the dirt off our hands and made lunch. By the time we were finished eating, the woman next door had vanished. She had appeared to have something wrong with her, but apparently no one knew anything about her. At least Leslie could see her, so she wasn't a ghost. Many things consumed my mind about the woman. I went to bed later that night thinking about her. I wanted to know more of who she was, and became very determined to do so soon.

Chapter 13

The island was beautiful and big. There were many beaches where my friends and I swam and played over the next few weeks. One day while wandering through the woods, we discovered a hidden swim hole that had a small waterfall. This became our private getaway spot. We were sure others probably knew about it, but never seen anyone there when we went.

One night at dinner, Leslie discussed a carnival that had traveled our way.

"Did you hear about the big carnival?" Leslie asked.

"I saw posters hanging around the island. What is it about?" I asked.

"It's a carnival that travels. They come around once a year. If you want, we can take the ferry into town and go." She replied.

"What is there to do?" I asked.

"Well, they have rides that they set up, and lots of food."

She replied.

"Sure, we can go." I said.

"I think some others from the island are going too. Maybe you will see some of your friends there." Leslie stated.

"Do you think the Family next door would go if we invite them?" I asked.

"Pepper, you know you're not supposed to bother them." She replied.

"I know. I just thought they would go if someone invited them." I said.

"I am sure they know about it. If they want to go, they will on their own." She said.

A few days later, we traveled by ferry to the carnival. I saw my friend Tara on the ferry also.

"Are you going to the carnival?" I asked.

"Yes." Tara replied.

"That's where I'm going too." I said.

"Have you ever been to one?" She asked.

"No." I replied.

"They are a lot of fun. I come every year. Maybe we can hang out at the carnival." She said.

"Okay." I said.

I returned to Leslie's side waiting anxiously to arrive at the carnival. My aunt agreed it would be fine to hang out with Tara and her mother while we were there. The first thing Tara wanted to do after arriving, was go through the clown house. I didn't know what to expect once I entered. Tara grabbed my hand and pulled me with her through a maze of mirrors. It took us awhile to find our way out, but we had a lot of fun.

We spent the rest of the day on different rides and eating. They made the best funnel cakes I had ever tasted. By the time we returned back to the island my belly was hurting. Leslie claimed it was just from all the sugar I had eaten throughout the day. I had no trouble sleeping that night after my big day at the carnival.

The next morning, I arose early. I stepped outside on the deck to enjoy the fresh morning air. As I gazed around, I saw the woman next door again. She appeared to be crying this time. I wanted to approach the woman to find out what was wrong, but I had promised Leslie, I wouldn't bother her. The woman was pacing back and forth in her back yard. I wandered what she could be crying about. Something or someone had made her sad. I felt discouraged that I couldn't help her. After an hour of pacing, the woman disappeared into her house. Leslie called me in for breakfast.

"I saw that woman next door again." I said.

"I told you to stay away from there." Leslie stated.

"I didn't go over. I could see her from the deck." I said.

"You shouldn't be nosy." She said.

"I can't help it. I'm curious about her. I saw her crying." I claimed.

"I'm sure she's fine." said Leslie.

"But what if she's not? What if she needs our help with something?" I asked.

"If she needs help, she will seek it." She replied.

"Maybe she doesn't know how." I said.

"Pepper, we need to mind our business around here. Everyone takes care of their own on this island." She said.

When I became upset, I left the kitchen to go outside for awhile. A few hours later, Leslie found me sitting under a tree in the woods.

"There you are." Leslie said.

"Yeah, so." I said glancing down at the ground.

"Pepper, I know mean good. But sometimes you have to just let things go." She said.

"I don't know what the big deal is about that family." I said.

"Not everyone wants to be known Pepper." She said.

"The woman comes outside a lot. Maybe her parents just don't want to be known." I said.

"Look, if she speaks to you one day while you are out then you are allowed to talk with her. Now how about that slumber party we talked about before? Have you asked your

friends yet?" She asked.

"No." I replied.

"Well, let's go make some phone calls. I will talk to their parents to make sure it would be okay for them to stay next weekend." She said.

We proceeded back to the house. Leslie set everything up with the parents of a few friends. I never had a sleepover before, but Leslie reassured me it would be fun. During the next week, Leslie planned for the slumber party. We put together party decorations and baked treats. It was fun hanging out with my aunt.

Friday night came, the day before my party, and there were no signs of the woman next door. She must have been busy to not come outside all week. I didn't speak about her to Leslie anymore. My mind debated on ways I could get her attention the next time I saw her. I knew if I could get her to talk to me, then I would be able to somehow help her sadness. Thinking about the woman next door, I fell asleep late.

The day of my slumber party finally came. I felt extremely excited about it as my friends began to arrive.

Everyone was amused with all the party decorations I hung up around Leslie's house.

"Did you do these yourself?" Jill asked as she glanced around.

"My aunt helped me put them together, but I hung them all." I replied.

"These are nice Pepper!" Jan excitedly said.

"Thank you!" I said back.

"You will have to come help me next time I have a party." claimed Chloe.

"Okay. Let's play some games." I said.

Over the next few hours, we played party games and danced on Leslie's deck. We were having so much fun that we almost forgot about all of the snacks we had.

"Are you girls ready for snacks yet?" Leslie asked.

"Yes!" We all yelled together.

"Come get them." Leslie said.

"Let's go!" I said excitedly to the other girls.

We quickly piled in the house to eat our snacks. We ate pizza, chips, cookies, cupcakes, and ice cream. Our bellies were so full that we returned to the deck to relax. We chatted till dark, and then went inside for a pillow fight. After over exhausting ourselves, we called it a night. Everyone got out their sleeping bags and found a spot in my room to sleep. As I lay on my bed, I thought about all the fun I had during the party while trying to sleep.

A few days later while walking home from school with my friends, we came across the island's graveyard. My friends began to play around the entrance of the graveyard while I watched from a distance.

"What's wrong Pepper?" asked Jan.

"I don't want to play near the graveyard." I replied.

"Why not?" Jan asked.

"She's scared." said Chloe.

"I'm not scared!" I angrily said.

"Then why won't you come in?" asked Jill.

204

"I just don't want to." I replied.

"Leave her alone. She doesn't have to play in the graveyard." Tara said meanly.

"Let's play hide and seek." said Jan.

"Yeah Pepper. Do you want to play?" asked Chloe.

"Not in the graveyard." I replied.

"Hey, we can play at Pepper's house instead of playing in the graveyard." Tara said.

"Yeah. We can do that." I responded.

We scurried back toward Leslie's house. On the way, I thanked Tara for looking out for me. The other girls quickly got over the fact that I wouldn't enter the graveyard. I didn't want them to know about my past right away, even though I knew I couldn't hide it forever. I wasn't ready to share any information that I didn't have to.

After arriving at Leslie's, we rested on the deck to catch our breaths. As we were chatting, something suddenly caught my eye. I glanced over and saw the woman next door outside again.

"There she is again." I softly stated.

"Who?" asked Chloe.

"The woman next door." I said while pointing.

Everyone turned to look.

"What is she doing?" asked Jan.

"It looks like she is ripping something up." said Tara.

"Does anyone know her name?" I asked.

"No." everyone replied.

"It looks like she's crying now." said Chloe.

"We should go see what's wrong." Jan said.

"No. I promised my aunt I wouldn't bother her" I responded.

"Come on Pepper. Don't be scared again." said Jill.

"I'm not scared!" I whispered loudly.

"Shhh! Look. She is going inside now." said Tara.

"Let's sneak over there and find out what she was

doing." Jan said.

"Maybe we shouldn't." I responded.

"Well, I'm going. You can stay here if you want." Jan said as she walked away.

"I'm going too." said the other girls as they tip-toed behind Jan.

Even though Leslie told me not to bother anyone, I chose to follow the other girls. We slowly made our way to the neighbor's yard. Chloe sat by a tree to keep watch. If anyone appeared, then Chloe would let us know. The rest of us crawled through the yard to where the woman was.

"Here is what she was ripping up." said Jan.

"What is it?" I asked.

"It looks like a picture of someone." Jill replied.

After glancing at the ripped picture for a few moments, I became curious about why the woman tore the picture up. As I picked up the pieces of the ripped picture, I put them in my pocket. All of a sudden, the mother came outside.

"Hey! What are you girls doing over here?" yelled the mother of the woman.

We jumped up and ran quickly back to Leslie's house. We were frightened and breathing heavily.

"What are you girls doing?" asked Leslie.

"Nothing." We all said together.

"Pepper, we should go now." Tara said as the girls began to walk away.

"Is anything wrong?" asked Leslie.

"No." I replied.

The phone began to ring, so Leslie went back into the house to answer it. A few minutes later, I saw the police approach the neighbor's house. I became scared and ran to my room. After awhile, I heard Leslie chatting with someone in the other room.

"Pepper!" Leslie called.

"Yes." I responded.

"Come here please." She said.

I approached Leslie slowly.

"Yes, aunt Leslie." I said.

"Were you and your friends next door?" Leslie asked.

I stood frightened to answer.

"Were you?" She asked.

"Yes." I replied.

"Why?" She asked.

"We saw the woman crying and ripping something up. We just wanted to see what it was." I replied.

"Young lady, I have been notified that she doesn't want you back over there. If you are caught again, you will get charged with trespassing. Do you understand?" a police officer interrupted.

"Yes." I responded.

"Go to your room. I will be in there to talk to you in a minute." Leslie said.

As I walked away, Leslie turned to the officer to assure

him I wouldn't be bothering anyone anymore. Breaking my promise with Leslie, I felt guilty. I wasn't sure what my punishment would be, but I didn't care either. My curious temptations of others grew difficult to resist.

About a half hour later, Leslie entered my room and sat on my bed next to me.

"I know I promised you I wouldn't bother anyone." I said sadly.

"Yes, you did." Leslie responded.

"I'm sorry." I said.

"Do you realize how much trouble you are going to get yourself in if you keep going back over there?" Leslie asked.

"Yes." I replied.

"I know you are curious, but I told you they don't like to associate with others." Leslie said.

"I know." I responded.

Well, I want you to come straight home after school everyday for the next few weeks. Maybe being away from your friends will keep you out of trouble for awhile. I am sure they will be in trouble also. The police are paying their parents a visit too." said Leslie.

"Okay." I said.

I went to bed early, but I couldn't sleep much because my attention was on the scary looking mother next door. She had scars on her face, like she had been cut with a knife. She had bruises on her arms and a crooked nose. Her eyebrows were thick and her eyes were dark. She appeared as if she had evil living within her. I was frightened by the image in my mind. After a few hours, I finally found enough peace of mind that I could go to sleep.

The next few weeks appeared to be going by slowly. I minded what Leslie said and came straight home from school everyday. A few friends at school were upset about getting into trouble so I left them alone. Tara was the only one that would speak to me without blaming me for what happened. One day at school I asked her about it.

"How come everyone is mad at me?" I asked.

"Don't pay attention to them." Tara replied.

"I try not to." I said.

"Hey, when we are finished with our punishments we can go to the waterfall in the woods and hang out." said Tara.

"Yeah. Okay." I responded.

To make time seem faster, I watched the house next door and took notes of everything I saw. One night, I heard muffled screaming coming from inside the house. I wandered what could be happening over there. Whatever it was, I didn't feel that it was good. Eventually, I decided I was going to start leaving notes to get the woman's attention, but I knew if anyone caught me, I would be in deep trouble. The decision was made to leave the notes at night, so I wouldn't get caught. I wrote short positive notes to begin with. Then, I slipped out at night to quickly leave the note, before returning back to my room. Each day I watched the woman read the notes and gaze around.

After my punishment was over, I began to prepare a surprise for the woman next door. I worked on taping the torn picture I brought home the day I was caught at her house. After I fixed it, I thought it would be nice to return it to her. It ended up being a picture of a newborn baby when I finished it. The reasons as to why she wanted to tear it up, confused me.

Chapter 14

As I relaxed in bed, I gazed at the picture of the baby until I fell asleep. When I arose from a long nap, I began to plan how I would return the picture to the woman. The next few months went by fast. I had seen no signs of the odd woman or her family. It was like, they had vanished from the island. I stared at their house daily as I sat on the deck outside, but no sounds were noticeable from anyone next door. It was odd and I wandered if everything was okay with the woman. I remained quiet at dinner with the woman on my mind.

"What is the matter Pepper?" asked Leslie.

"Nothing." I replied.

"You have been quiet for the last few weeks." Leslie stated.

"I am just thinking about the woman next door." I said.

"Why are you thinking about that again?" She asked.

"I haven't seen her lately." I replied.

"So..." Leslie stated curiously.

"So, don't you find that strange?" I asked.

"No, I don't." She replied bluntly.

"Why not?" I asked.

"Pepper, no one barely sees them anyway. Nobody finds it strange." She replied.

"Well, maybe something is wrong." I stated.

"Nothing is wrong over there. They just don't want to be bothered." She said.

"I find it strange that they don't want to be known." I said.

"There is nothing strange about wanting to be left alone." Leslie said.

"Could we make the woman a pie or something and take it to her?" I asked.

"No." Leslie replied quickly.

"But, it's a nice thing to do... and we could meet them that way." I stated.

"Pepper, we are not going to go over there. You heard what the police said. You have to stay away from there." She said.

I sat and finished my dinner in silence. After I cleaned my plate over the sink, I approached Leslie one more time.

"What happened to the old woman?" I asked.

"What do you mean?" Leslie quickly asked back.

"Well, have you seen her lately?" I asked.

"A few times around town." She replied.

"She looks all cut up... and I think her nose is broke." I stated.

"She has scars on her, and her nose is not broke." Leslie said giggling.

"It looks broke. Is she a witch?" I asked curiously.

"No, she is not. You should go clean your room now and get ready for bed soon." Leslie replied.

"Okay." I said.

"Goodnight." She said as I walked away.

Slowly, I cleaned my room with the mysterious woman on my mind. I didn't know why I was so fascinated in her. It seemed as if there were some kinds of connection to her somehow. After finishing my room, I climbed into bed. It wasn't long before I fell asleep and was awakened by the bright morning sun shining into my eyes. Quickly, I dressed myself and ran to the kitchen for breakfast.

It was a beautiful morning, so I decided to eat breakfast outside on the deck. While enjoying the nice breeze, all of a sudden, a close noise startled me. I turned around quickly to observe my surroundings. It had appeared the mysterious woman decided to finally come out of hiding. She stared at me as I stood with my mouth ajar. The long eye contact had me in disbelief. It seemed as if we connected eyes for minutes, neither one of us moving an inch.

"Pepper!" Leslie called.

"Yes, aunt Leslie." I said in a startling voice as I turned back around.

"Did I scare you?" Leslie asked as she approached the

door.

"No. I am fine." I replied.

"What are you doing?" She asked curiously.

"I was just... uh. enjoying the amazing views from the deck. That's all." I replied.

"Well, I am going out for awhile. Will you be okay here by yourself for awhile?" She asked.

"Yes, I will be fine." I replied.

"Okay. I will see you when I return. I shouldn't be long." Leslie said as she walked away.

I glanced behind me, but the strange woman had disappeared. I sat down nervously to finish my breakfast. After eating, I decided to sneak around the neighbor's house. Before walking slowly to the edge of Leslie's yard, I grabbed the picture of the baby the woman had torn up. There were no signs of the strange woman next door. I crawled up toward her house in fear of getting caught again.

"Hey!" someone shouted.

"*Yes.*" I quickly replied in fear as I jumped to a sitting position on the ground.

"*What are you doing here.*" The strange woman asked as I sat staring at her.

"*I... I...*" I stuttered to reply.

"*You know my mother is going to be upset if she catches you here?*" The woman stated.

"*I'm sorry.*" I replied.

"*So, what do you want?*" She asked.

"*I wanted to give you this back.*" I replied as I handed her the picture I fixed.

"*Where did you get this?*" She asked.

"*I watched you tear it up, so I came over to get it.*" I replied as the woman zoned into the picture.

"*Why did you fix it?*" The woman sadly asked.

"*You seemed sad and I wanted to make you feel better. Who is the baby I the picture?*" I asked curiously.

"It's my daughter." She replied.

"Why would you tear a picture of your daughter up?" I asked.

"I have been angry because I haven't seen my daughter since birth. I don't know that I would ever be able to find her now." the woman replied.

"Did she go missing?" I asked.

"No. I gave her away at birth. She must think I'm a bad person." She replied.

"Is this the only picture you had of her?" I asked.

"Hold on, I will be right back." She replied as she walked into her house.

After a few minutes of waiting, the woman finally returned. She had a handful of pictures in her hand.

"Here are the pictures I have from my pregnancy with her ... and a few of her after she was born." The woman said as she handed me the pictures slowly.

As I scrounged through the pictures the woman handed

me, one caught my eye. I saw pictures of her while pregnant and pictures of her with the baby after birth, but one picture stood out more than the others. It was a picture of the woman wearing a necklace that was similar to the one I picked up at the graveyard back in the city.

"What is this?" I asked while pointing to the necklace in the picture.

"That is a necklace that was handed down to me by my grandmother." The woman replied.

"Where is it now?" I asked softly.

"I left it with my daughter when I gave her away." She replied.

At that moment I gasped for a breath.

"What is wrong?" The woman asked.

"Nothing, I got to go." I replied quickly as I ran away from her.

I scurried back to Leslie's house as fast as I could. Leslie shortly waked in after.

"What is wrong with you?" Leslie asked.

"Nothing." I replied quickly and out of breath.

"You look like you have just seen a ghost." She stated

"I am not feeling well. I will be in my room." I said as I walked away.

"Do you want lunch?" She asked.

"No!" I hollered back.

Curiously, I grabbed the necklace I had put up and observed it for hours. I couldn't help but think this was the same necklace as the one in the picture. How would I explain the reason for having it? There was no logical explanation except for that I stole it from her daughter's grave. I knew she would become angry with me if I told her, so I came to the conclusion that I would avoid the woman and never talk to her again. Then I wouldn't have to tell her.

Over the next few months, it grew colder outside. According to Leslie, the winters on the island wasn't near as bad as they were in the city. A few times, I seen the woman next door, but I hid from her when she came out. There was no way I could face her with everything I knew. I continued my days as normal as possible over the winter months avoiding the woman next door as much as I could.

One night at dinner, Leslie questioned me.

"How come you been spending so much time inside lately?" Leslie asked.

"I just haven't felt like going out much." I replied.

"Is everything okay?" She asked.

"Yes." I replied.

"Have you seen the lady next door lately?" She asked sarcastically.

"Not really. Why do you ask?" I asked back.

"Just curious. You were always interested in her before." She replied.

"I don't want to talk about her anymore." I said firmly.

"Did something happen?" She asked.

"No." I replied quickly.

We continued dinner glancing at each other as if we didn't know what else to talk about. After dinner, I took the necklace outside and thought about what to do. I began to think the best thing to do is bury the necklace and leave things alone. As I sat in thought, two feet stepped in front of me. I slowly looked up nervously at the person. It was the strange woman from next door. Frightened, my heart started to race.

"Why have you been avoiding me?" She asked curiously.

"I don't know." I replied in fear.

"Yes, you do. You purposely ran away from me when I told you about the necklace in the picture and then every time, I see you...." She stated before getting interrupted.

"Okay... okay..." I rudely interrupted. *"Here!"* I said as I handed her the necklace.

"What is this for?" She asked.

"It's a necklace. Like the one in the picture." I replied.

The woman stood silently with the night wind blowing through her hair. After a long few minutes of waiting, she finally spoke softly.

"My parents made me do it." She stated.

"Do what?" I asked.

"Made me give my baby away." She replied sadly.

"Oh." I softly said.

"My parents were strict people. When they found out I was pregnant, they grew angry with me." She said.

"They could have helped you." I said.

"I had to hide my pregnancy from others." She went on to explain.

"Why?" I asked.

"They said I was a disgrace to the family for getting pregnant before marriage they were embarrassed, and didn't want anyone to know. When the baby was born, they took me to drop her off at her father's." She explained.

"I know." I said.

"What did you say?" She asked.

"I know." I replied.

"How do you know anything?" She asked angrily.

"Pepper!" Leslie called.

"I will be right in." I said back to Leslie.

I jumped to my feet and politely snatched the necklace from the woman's hand.

"I have to go." I said.

"What is it that you know?" She asked.

"I will talk to you soon about it." I replied as I walked away.

It was not long before I hopped into bed with the necklace in my hand. As I lay in the dark, an uneasy feeling came over me. I began to tremble as thoughts of the strange woman raced through my mind. Finally, I reached the decision to be truthful with her about everything I knew.

After a few short days, I had another encounter with the woman. As I arrived home from school, she was pacing in front of Leslie's house. I slowly approached her.

"I haven't seen you around the last few days." The woman stated.

"I have been busy." I said.

"I think you have something to tell me." She said.

"Yes, I do." I said.

"I'm listening." She said.

"I moved here from the city. Sometime after my mom died, I went to visit her grave one day and stumbled across a necklace." I said.

"The necklace you showed me the other night?" She asked.

"Yes." I replied.

"I know it's the same necklace I gave to my daughter. I have been wandering how you would of got a hold of it. At first, I thought maybe you and my daughter were friends at some point and she gave it to you. But now you are telling me you found it in a graveyard?" She asked.

"Yes." I replied.

"Well, my daughter must have dropped it there. I can go find her and return it to her." She stated.

"No, you can't." I blurted out.

"No?" She curiously asked.

"You don't understand." I replied.

"Understand what?" She asked.

"That your daughter is dead!" I exclaimed.

The woman gasped and didn't speak a word as she gave me a look of shock.

"I'm sorry." I said softly.

"You must be talking about the wrong baby." She said in disbelief.

"No. I saw the name on her grave. I went to research information about her and I found out she was killed by her father." I said.

"It can't be true." She said.

"Her uncle told me the story of you leaving her at birth."

I said.

"If this is true, then why would you steal her necklace?" She asked.

"I didn't steal the necklace. I found it on the ground near her grave and thought someone must of dropped it." I explained.

"This is all my fault." The woman said.

"No, it's not." I said back.

"If I wouldn't have left her, she would still be alive." She claimed.

"You didn't have a choice. Your parents made you do it." I said.

"I should have fought against it. I should of ran away with her." She said.

"You can't change things now." I said.

The woman busted out into tears. I didn't know what else to say to her. I stood with my head down in shame that I couldn't help her. She eventually ambled away in tears. Aunt

Leslie arrived home to find me seated on her steps outside.

"Is everything okay?" Leslie asked.

"Yes." I replied.

"You seem a little sad about something. Do you want to talk about it?" She asked.

"No." I replied.

"Well, I am going to go make dinner. If you want to talk later, I will be here." She said as she walked into the house.

Leslie went inside the house to cook while I stayed outside. After dinner was finished, I went inside to eat. I wasn't very hungry, so I nibbled at my food.

"Okay, what is wrong with you?" Leslie asked.

"Nothing." I replied.

"Don't say nothing. You are hardly eating, and you haven't said a word since you sat down at the table." She stated.

"I'm just not that hungry tonight." I claimed.

"I'm not buying that. Talk to me." She said.

"I don't want to talk about it!" I said angrily as I stomped to my room.

Being upset, I spent the rest of my evening in my room because I did not want to see or talk to anyone. All I could do is lye on my bed like a paralyzed vegetable, thinking about the woman next door. I knew how she felt inside with the sadness that death brought. The day fell into darkness and I eventually fell asleep.

Chapter 15

At school the next day, Tara approached me. She noticed I wasn't my usual self. With everything that was running through my little mind, how could I be normal. I wanted to find a way to make the strange woman feel better. It was difficult for me to see anyone that sad. I wasn't up for a conversation with Tara, but she wouldn't leave me alone about it.

"What is wrong?" Tara asked.

"I'm sad today." I replied...

"Why?" She asked.

"I been talking to that neighbor woman. The one who tore the picture up." I replied.

"Pepper! You will get in trouble." said Tara.

"No, it's fine. She talks to me now." I said.

"But you were told to stay away them." Tara claimed.

"I know, but I was too curious to stay away." I said.

"Come on girl's, you are going to be ate for class." said a teacher in the hallway.

"I will talk to you at lunch." I said as I walked away.

The first half of the school day seemed the longest. I didn't pay attention in class, but instead twiddled my thumbs on a loaded mind. The teacher gave out a writing assignment. We each had to hand write a one-page paper about our family. The topic could be of our choice from what our family liked to do, to what we liked best about our family. We could write anything we wanted as long as it pertained to our family. The teacher gave us a week for the assignment, in which then we would share our own writing to the class. This was going to be difficult for me to do since my family was either dead or in jail. I thought I would talk to Leslie later to get some ideas.

At lunch, Tara clung to me like never before.

"So, tell me more about the woman next door." Tara said.

"Why are you so curious all of a sudden?" I asked.

"You already told me you been talking to her, so tell me what she is like." She replied.

"She's nice." I said.

"Nice? That's all you can say?" She asked.

"Well, I did find out that this necklace I found back in the city belongs to her dead daughter." I replied.

"I didn't know she had a daughter." She said.

"Yes, her parents made her give the baby away when she was born, so she gave her to the father. The father ended up killing her a few years later." I said.

"You are lying. Where did you hear that from?" asked Tara.

"I'm not lying. I went to visit my mom's grave one day and stumbled across her daughter's grave. Then I searched to find out what happened to her. I found out her father killed her." I replied.

"Maybe it's not her daughter." She stated.

"Yes, it was. She left a necklace with her baby. I found the necklace at the graveyard that day. And she has a picture with the necklace on while she was pregnant." I said.

"Lunch is over!" yelled the lunch lady from afar.

"Better be careful." Tara said.

"Why?" I asked.

"I don't want anything to happen to you." She replied as she walked away.

Later that night, I thought of the time I had an imaginary friend at Grandma's house. I recalled when she told me about her father not wanting her, and she couldn't find her mother, as well as her following me from the city. I began to think she was Cherry from the graveyard. Reasons of why she would be following me flowed through my mind as I tried to sleep.

The next evening, I ran into the woman next door again. I approached her with conversation.

"Sorry about your daughter." I said.

She ignored me, as if I weren't there.

"Do you believe in ghosts?" I asked.

She looked at me in an astonished way.

"Why do you ask?" The woman asked.

"I think your daughter has been following me." I replied.

"What do you mean?" She asked.

The woman sat silently to listen while I explain why I thought her dead daughter had been following me. I told her about the imaginary friend I had at Grandma's and how she had followed me from the city.

"Can you see her now?" The woman asked.

"No. I haven't seen her since I left Grandma's, but I have started hearing things again. I think it's her." I replied.

"What kind of things do you hear?" She asked.

"While lying in bed one night, I held the necklace in my hand. I heard noises, like someone was in the room." I replied.

"Well it was probably nothing." She said.

She continued on about her business while I watched confused.

"You must not believe me." I said after a few minutes.

"I believe in ghosts. I am just not sure my daughter is following you." She stated.

"Maybe it's the necklace." I said.

"You mean my necklace?" She asked.

I glared at her for a moment.

"Technically speaking, You did take the necklace I gave my daughter. It did belong to me." She said.

"You are right. Here, you can have it back." I said as I handed the necklace back to the woman.

The woman gently took the necklace. She stared at it for awhile as I observed her face. She looked as if she wanted to cry again.

"I'm sorry I took the necklace." I said softly.

"It's okay, you didn't know." The woman said.

"You love it a lot, I'm guessing by the way you are looking at it." I said.

"Yes, it has been in the family for some time now." She said.

"I am sure your daughter loved it just as much." I said.

"My mother became upset with me when she found out I left it with her." The woman said after a moment.

"Why?" I asked.

"My daughter meant nothing to her. She was ashamed of her." She sadly replied.

"I know where your daughter is buried." I said.

"Was it the same graveyard as your mother?" She asked.

"Yes, It's back in the city." I replied.

"We should return the necklace to my daughter." She said.

"How would we do that?" I asked.

"We can go to the city and bury the necklace on my daughter's grave." She replied.

"Yes, then she will stop following me and be happy." I said.

"Will you show me where her grave is?" The woman asked.

"Wait! I don't know if I should go. I mean, my aunt will be mad if I leave the island by myself." I said.

"You won't be by yourself. I will be with you." She said.

"My aunt would never allow it." I said.

"You have to go with me. I need you to go." The woman pleaded.

"I will talk to you later about it. I have to go for now." I said as I ran away.

Over the next few days, I avoided the woman next door. I didn't want to leave the island and chance making my aunt upset, but I wanted to help the woman get to her daughter's grave. I couldn't sleep much at night or think clearly during the day due to my big decision I had to make.

Tara questioned me daily at school about the woman,

but I chose not to talk much about her to Tara yet. I knew if I told her anything, she would try to talk me out of leaving the island, so I wanted time to make the decision on my own. I would discuss my plans with Tara once I made up my mind.

The weekend finally came, and Leslie wanted me to go out with her. We were gone most of the day running errands. Leslie decided to stop at a small diner on the island for dinner on the way home. We ordered food and sat to eat.

"How has school been?" asked Leslie.

"Good." I replied

"Someone mentioned they saw you with the woman next door." She said.

"We are friends now." I said.

"Friends?" She asked curiously.

"Yes, we have been talking for a few weeks or so now." I replied.

"Pepper, I really don't know much about them. You could get in trouble if you are caught over there again. You know what the police said." Leslie said.

240

"Her mother doesn't know we talk." I said.

"I am still concerned about you." She said.

"Don't be. I will be fine." I said.

"What do you two talk about?" She asked.

"Her daughter mostly." I replied.

"I didn't know she had a daughter." Leslie said.

"No one does, and you can't tell anyone. Her mother made her give the baby away when she was born." I said.

"She told you this?" She asked.

"Yes, she showed me pictures too." I replied.

"Where is her daughter now?" asked Leslie.

"I told her that her daughter was dead." I replied softly.

"Now why would you say something like that?" She asked.

"Cause it's the truth." I replied.

"How would you know that Pepper?" She asked.

"It's a long story, but I found out in the city before I came." I replied.

"I have plenty of time to listen." She said.

"Maybe some other time." I said.

After returning home, I went to my room for the night. I imagined what my life would be like if Red were still here. I had missed my family every day. Even though Frank had become evil, I thought about him also. Leslie was nice, but I missed the old days with Isabelle, Frank, and Red.

The next morning, I went to talk to the woman next door. She was outside early, so I approached her.

"Hi." I said.

"Hello." She said.

"What are you doing?" I asked.

"Planning a trip to the city." She replied.

"I have decided to go with you." I said.

"Really?" She asked.

"Yes, I want to help you." I replied.

"We can't tell anyone. If we do, they will try to stop us." The woman said.

"I won't tell anyone." I said as I crossed my fingers behind my back.

"I figure we could leave at night. The last ferry leaves at eight." She said.

"How am I going to leave without my aunt knowing?" I asked.

"Tell her you are going to bed early, and then sneak out. She won't know your gone till the next morning. We will be far gone by then." She replied.

"What if she catches me sneaking out?" I asked.

"She won't if you are quiet." She replied.

"When will we leave?" I asked.

"Next Friday. My mom is going to be out of town for the weekend. We will leave then." She replied.

"Okay. Next Friday at eight. I will come here and we

can leave together." I said.

"No, we can't be seen together. Meet me at the ferry next Friday." She said.

"Okay, I will be there at eight. I have to go." I said as I walked away.

The remainder of the day I thought about my decision I had made. I had to come up with another way of sneaking around without Leslie finding out. Maybe I should tell her I am staying with Tara for the weekend so she will never know I left the island. We had only planned on being gone for a couple days. I decided I should ask Tara to cover for me.

In school the following Monday, I told Tara I needed to talk to her about something important. She agreed we could talk after school on the way home. I knew she would be against my decision, but I wanted her to cover for me. I thought she would be the only one who would. The school day went fast for me. I met up with Tara so we could walk home together.

"So, what is it you want to talk to me about?" Tara asked.

"I am going to leave the island." I replied.

"You are moving?" She asked.

"No... The woman next door wants to go to the city for something, and I am going with her." I replied.

"Are you nuts?!" Tara asked in a loud voice.

"I am just going to help her get somewhere. She doesn't know her way around the city. We are only going to gone a couple days." I replied.

"Your aunt will never go for that." Tara said.

"I'm not going to tell her." I said.

"She will know you are gone." She said.

"I'm going to tell her I will be at your house for the weekend." I said.

"No, you are not putting me in the middle of this one." Tara said.

"You don't have to say anything. She will just think I'm at your house and I will be back before the weekend is over." I said.

"I don't think that will work." She said.

"It will if you don't tell anyone." I said.

"I don't think you should go." Tara said.

"Why not?" I asked.

"The city can be dangerous, and I can't believe you want to go with that strange woman." Tara replied.

"She's a nice person. She just has mean parents." I said.

"I just don't think it's safe. I'm going to worry about you." She said.

"I won't be gone long, and I know the city well. There is nothing to worry about. Please promise me you won't say anything" I said.

"Okay. Please be careful." She said as we approached home.

I waited a few days before talking to Leslie about staying with Tara for the weekend. That whole week I was nervous about leaving the island. I had everything planned out and ready to go. I approached Leslie after dinner one night to discuss my plans to stay with Tara.

"Tara is wanting me to hang out this weekend." I said.

"That's good." Leslie said.

"I figured I could just stay with her this weekend." I said.

"The whole weekend?" Leslie asked.

"Yes, her parents are fine with it." I replied.

"Well, I guess if they are okay with it then you can go." She said.

"Okay, thanks." I said.

"What all are you going to do together?" Leslie asked.

"Just hang out on the island." I replied.

"Don't be out getting into trouble." She said.

"I'm not." I said.

"Maybe next weekend she can stay with you. I can call her mother and ask." She said.

"I can ask while I'm there this weekend. I am sure her mother won't mind her staying next weekend." I said.

"Okay. Well get some sleep. You have school tomorrow, and a big weekend ahead of you." said Leslie.

"Good night." I said as I walked to my room.

At school the next day, I filled Tara in about everything being ready to go. I told her I had already talked to Leslie and she thought I would be at her house. Tara tried to talk me out of going with the woman to the city, but I had already made up my mind to go. I wasn't going to back out now. The woman was depending on me and I wasn't going to let her down.

Chapter 16

Friday night came, and I was more nervous than ever. Before packing a few things for the trip, I informed Leslie I was going to Tara's house for dinner. I knew I couldn't take a lot because Leslie would question me. Being sneaky had become my normal during this time. So, I could hide my face from others on the way to the ferry, I wore a hooded coat. After telling Leslie goodbye, I left for my mini adventure to the big city.

During the stroll around the island toward the ferry, I became overly freaked that someone would recognize me. Hiding my face, the best I could without being suspicious to others, it felt like everyone I passed were looking at me. I didn't think I would make it to the ferry without being caught.

When I finally arrived at the ferry, the woman from next door approached me quickly.

"Follow me, and act normal." The woman said quietly.

I followed her onto the ferry not saying a word. The man controlling the ferry glanced at us with one brow raised, but didn't speak. Surely, I thought we were caught. The old man started the ferry and drove toward the city. The woman and I sat cuddled near each other waiting to arrive in the city.

"That was close." I said

"We weren't going to get caught." The woman said with confidence.

"So, what's your name anyway?" I asked.

"Marla." She replied.

"My name is Pepper." I said.

"That's pretty. My daughter would have liked you." She said.

"I think she does already." I said.

"I meant you two would have been good friends in life." She said.

We were silent the rest of the trip. When we arrived to the city, I followed Marla off the ferry. We had to find somewhere to stay for the night. Marla took me behind a road long of restaurants where we settled for the night.

The next morning, I questioned Marla.

"What are we going to do now?" I asked.

"We are going to hitch a ride with someone." She replied.

"Who?" I asked.

"I don't know yet. Just sit still till I find someone." Marla said as she walked away.

I see Marla talking to a few people before coming to get me.

"Come on. I found us a ride." She said.

An old woman drove us the long journey back to where I came from. I kept quiet so I wouldn't upset Marla. After we were dropped off, I took Marla to the woods where I stayed a night when I ran away from the big facility.

"We can stay here tonight in this tree house. I have stayed here before. No one will find us." I said.

"Okay. We will come back here later. Let's go find the grave yard." Marla said.

Marla followed me as I walked toward the graveyard. I continued to hide my face, so no one would recognize me from the city. After arriving at the graveyard, I escorted Marla in. we slowly scuffled toward Cherry's grave. Marla stood in front her grave for awhile. She finally fell to the ground in tears as she started to dig at the dirt by Cherry's headstone.

"What are you doing?" I asked Marla

"I am going to bury the necklace here, so no one takes it again." She replied.

I took watch as Marla buried the necklace on Cherry's grave. I didn't want to be caught disturbing anyone's grave. After she finished, we stayed for awhile longer.

"I miss her a lot." Marla said.

"I know." I said.

"I regret giving her away. My life is full of regret." She said.

"It's not your fault." I said.

"There hasn't been a day that I haven't thought about her." She said.

"You can't go back and change anything." I said.

She cried a little longer before we left. I stopped a minute on the way out to visit Red and Isabelle's grave.

"Is this your mother's grave?" Marla asked.

"Yes, and that's my brother's grave over there." I replied pointing at Red's grave.

"How did they die?" She asked.

"They were killed." I replied.

"Oh, sorry." said Marla.

"Yeah, we have something in common." I said.

We ventured back to the woods after stopping to eat. I wouldn't be scared to sleep in the tree house since I had someone else staying with me. Marla and I climbed the tree to settle in for the night. As we lye in the dark together, I began a conversation.

"I met her uncle." I said.

"Who's uncle?" asked Marla.

"Cherry's." I replied.

"Oh." She said.

"We talked awhile in the park one day." I said.

"What did you talk about?" Marla asked.

"How Cherry died." I replied.

"It makes me angry to think about it." She said.

"I found out he was dead, the uncle." I said.

"What do you mean he was dead?" She asked.

"I can see and talk to dead people." I replied.

"Are you saying he was dead when he told you about Cherry?" Marla asked.

"Yes." I replied.

Marla became silent.

"He told me Cherry's dad is in jail, here in the city." I said.

"I should go see him." Marla said.

"Why would you want to go see him?" I asked.

"I want him to look me eye to eye and tell me how he could kill our daughter," She replied.

"Did you know he was a killer?" I asked.

"No, he didn't seem like that type of person when we were sneaking around." She replied.

"From what the uncle told me; I think he might have been depressed." I said.

"Maybe it's my fault for that too. I mean, I did leave our daughter for him to raise alone." She said.

"You can't keep walking around blaming yourself for everything that happened." I said.

"I need to go see him to see what happened." She said.

"But we are supposed to go back to the island tomorrow." I said.

"We need to stay a few more days." She said.

"I will get in trouble." I said.

"I don't want to stay alone." She said.

"My aunt thinks I'm at a friend's house for the weekend. She is expecting me back tomorrow." I said.

"Please stay with me." She pleaded.

"I don't know if I can." I said.

"Just a couple more days." She pleaded again.

"I will let you know in the morning." I said.

Morning approached quickly and I still wasn't sure what to do. I didn't want to upset Leslie, but I felt sorry for Marla. I knew I would probably stay and help because that was the type of person I was. When Marla woke up, I told her I would help her. I wanted her to be at peace with everything.

"Thank you for staying with me." Marla said.

"I have to go back in a couple more days." I said.

"I know. I will take you back." She said.

"I will take you to the jail today, but I won't go in." I said.

"*I should go in and just hurt him like he did my baby girl.*" Marla stated.

"*You can't do that. He will be behind bars anyway.*" I said.

"*I can try to find a way to get to him.*" She said.

"*You will go to jail if you try it.*" I said.

"*Yes, I guess you are right. I just feel so much anger toward him the more I think about my daughter.*" She said.

"*I know you do, but you can't go in doing stupid things.*" I said.

We decided to go eat and walk in the park before visiting the jail. We sat at the same place I found out about Cherry. The park was packed with people and kids. It turned out to be a beautiful day. Families were everywhere. Marla and I sat gazing around.

"*Wish my family were here again.*" I said.

"*I bet your family were nice.*" Marla said.

"*My mom was very nice. I looked up to her. She was*

more beautiful than any woman I've known." I said.

"Was it her beauty that killed her?" She asked.

"What do you mean?" I asked.

"Well, some guys get so jealous over women that are beautiful that if they feel they are going to lose them they will just kill them." She replied.

"I never thought of it that way, but I think my dad was jealous... And I heard that my mom had asked for a divorce." I said.

"Yeah, I would say her beauty killed her." She said.

"I didn't like the way she suffered." I said.

"How's that?" She asked.

"My father slowly killed her with poison over a few years." I replied.

"Are you kidding?" She asked.

"No. All that time we just thought she was sick with something the doctors couldn't figure out." I replied.

"That is a horrible way to die." She said.

"Yes, I was angry at my father for a long time." I said.

"How did you finally find out it was poison that killed her?" She asked.

"My brother found out and kept it a secret. I found his diary one day and read it. That's how I found out... But my father found out that Red knew about it, and killed him to keep him silent. Then I told the police about the diary that exposed everything. Now my father is in jail." I replied.

"Oh my, you have been through a terrible life." She said.

"It wasn't always bad. I have a lot of good memories that I hold on to." I said.

"Where is the rest of your family?" She asked.

"I don't have any. I lived with my grandma for awhile before she died of old age. Other than that, I have a few cousins and I live with my aunt." I replied.

"That's just as sad as my life." She said.

"Why is your mother so mean?" I asked.

"She has always been that way. She is a strict parent. I had to sneak around a lot when I was younger. She wouldn't allow me to do much." She replied.

"What about your dad?" I asked.

"I never saw my father much. He worked all day and I was in bed before he arrived home." She replied.

"Where is your dad now?" I asked.

"He is home. He lets her be in control. He doesn't go out much anymore. I was actually surprised they took a trip this weekend." She replied.

"Where did they go?" I asked.

"Mom said something about Dad needing to go for doctor care out of town. I don't really care. If I had it my way, I would leave home and never return." She replied.

"You can leave home. You are old enough now." I said.

"And go where?" She asked.

"I don't know." I replied.

"I have nowhere to go and my mother has forever ruined my life when she made me give my baby up." She said.

"Your life isn't over. You could move in with someone else and work on having a better life. Do you have other family?" I asked.

"If I do then I don't know them." She replied.

"Oh." I said.

"We should run away together and be happy." Marla implied.

"I can't do that. The police would search for me." I said.

"Yeah." She said sadly.

"When I get old enough, we can." I said.

"I don't feel up to going to the jail today. Can we go tomorrow instead?" She asked.

"Yes, that's fine." I replied.

"We can go back to the woods to sleep again." She said.

"Okay." I said.

After spending most of the day at the park, we headed back to the woods for the night. On the way back, we walked past the facility I stayed in. I stopped for a minute.

"Are you okay?" Marla asked.

"This was the facility I stayed in while my father went through his trial." I replied.

"It doesn't look like a fun place." She said.

"No, it wasn't." I said.

Nervously, I glanced up at the window and noticed Mae looking down at me. Then, I hurried along quickly so she wouldn't recognize who I was. The rest of the way back, I thought about my life at the facility. I wanted to go visit, but I knew I couldn't. We turned in early so we could rest for tomorrow's journey.

The next day, Marla and I discussed our plans for the prison.

"I will walk you to the prison and wait outside for you." I said.

"Where will you be?" She asked.

"We can figure that out when we get there." I replied.

"I shouldn't be long." She said.

"It's fine. I will figure out where to hide so I am not seen." I said.

"What are we going to say if you are caught?" She asked.

"I will tell them I was helping you." I replied.

"Then I will get in trouble." She said.

"My aunt already knows I am with you." I said.

"How would she know that?" Marla asked.

"I told my friend Tara what I was doing." I replied.

"You weren't supposed to tell anyone." She said.

"I know but I wanted to tell Tara in case something happened to me." I said.

"You don't trust me?" She asked.

"Yes, I trust you, but I still wanted someone to know... And I'm sure Tara has told my aunt by now." I replied.

"So, guess I shouldn't go back." She said.

"You won't be in trouble. I will tell my aunt it was my idea to come to the city." I said.

"She won't believe it." said Marla.

"She will. I will make sure you don't get blamed for this." I said.

"Come on. We need to get to the jail." Marla said as she began to walk.

We didn't speak most of the way to the jail. I hid my face with the hood of my coat again. I became even more nervous as we got closer to the jail. We must have passed five police men on the way, but they didn't recognize me. After arriving to our destination, I searched for a place to hide out. I glanced around quickly and noticed a big field around the jail.

"I will have to go back down the street to hide." I said to Marla.

"Meet me at the coffee shop down the road in awhile." Marla said.

"Okay. I will go there and wait. Try to hurry." I said as I walked away.

Slowly, I walked to the coffee shop. Even though I didn't drink coffee, I sat to wait for Marla to return. It was warm inside the shop, but I was afraid to take my coat off in fear someone would know who I was. My face was probably on the news by now as a missing person and Leslie was freaking out. I thought of ways I could explain myself once I returned to the island, but nothing was going to be easy to explain anymore. Worried about Marla getting into trouble, I decided we should split up once the ferry arrived on the island.

It seemed as if I were there for hours when suddenly a police officer came in. My heart raced as I sat patiently. As he waited on his coffee, I noticed the police officer was glancing at me. Scared and alone, I wasn't sure if I should run or wait. After getting his coffee, the officer slowly left the store. The officer appeared to be on his phone as I glanced out the window. I decided to go out the side door of the coffee shop and wait for Marla behind the coffee shop, where I would be less noticeable.

Chapter 17

Marla finally decided to appear. I whistled for her to come behind the coffee shop.

"Why are you back here?" Marla asked.

"That cop out front seen me, so I came back here." I replied.

"We need to get out of here." She said.

"We will have to get out of here without the cop seeing us." I said.

"Follow me, and don't attract attention." She said.

We headed back toward the woods. The policeman was too busy drinking his coffee and reading the paper to notice us. On our way, I tried to get answers from Marla.

"What took you so long anyway?" I asked.

"They had me in questioning." She replied.

"Questioning for what?" I asked.

"They wanted to know who I was and how I knew Cherry's father." She replied.

"What did you tell them?" I asked.

"I told them the truth, that it was my daughter he killed and I had just found out." She replied.

"Did they ask why you left her with him?" I asked.

"I told them everything." She replied.

"Did they let you see him?" I asked.

"No." She replied.

"We did all this for nothing?" I asked.

"I will explain why later." She replied.

"Why can't you tell me now?" I asked.

"Look, we need to get back to the woods. We can't be seen together right now." She replied.

"What are you hiding from me?" I asked.

"I'm not hiding anything. I will talk to you later about it." She replied.

We approached the front of the woods where we had been hiding out. Marla glanced around to make sure no one had followed us there.

"You go to the tree house." Marla said.

"You are not coming?" I asked.

"I will be back." She replied.

"Where are you going?" I asked curiously.

"I'm going to find us some food." She replied.

"I can go help you." I said.

"No, I told you we can't be seen together." She said.

"Fine." I said as I walked into the woods.

"I will return soon with the food." She said.

As I returned to the tree house to wait, I wandered what happened when Marla went to the jail. I didn't like when people left me in the cold about things. Waiting on Marla to return, I became bored, so I decided to walk a little further into the woods. After walking a few minutes, I came to a small creek. While sitting on the bank of the creek, I threw tiny rocks into the water. Suddenly, it dawned on me that this must have been the creek the police found Red's body at. Becoming increasingly frightened, I ran back to the tree house.

As I approached the tree where we had been staying, I noticed Marla standing under it. She was glancing around nervously.

"What are you doing?" I asked.

"Waiting for you." She replied.

"You were gone a long time." I quietly said.

"Where did you go?" Marla asked.

"I got bored and took a walk." I replied.

"Find anything interesting?" She asked.

"I found the creek my brother was killed at." I replied.

"You hungry?" She asked to quickly change the subject.

"Sure." I replied.

We ate in silence as we watched the darkness fall. Marla appeared to be acting strange since she had left the jail. I wasn't sure if I should ask anymore questions.

"Well, we better get some rest. We have a long journey ahead of us tomorrow."

Marla said.

"About that, I was thinking it be a good idea if we split up once we got back on the ferry. So, you don't get in any trouble." I said.

"Yes, that's a good idea." She said.

We settled down on the tree house to rest, but I couldn't sleep. Marla appeared to be in deep thought staring into the darkness.

"I can't sleep." I said.

"Me either." Marla said.

"You never told me what happened at the jail today." I said.

"I am not sure where to start." She said.

271

"Why didn't they let you see him?" I asked.

"He wasn't there." She replied.

"He got out of jail?!" I asked surprised.

"No, he's dead." She replied.

"What happened?" I asked.

"They said he hung himself... Something about him being on laundry duty and used an old sheet to hang himself in one of the bathrooms near the laundry room." She replied.

"I don't know what to say." I said.

"The police said no one liked him in prison anyway." She said.

"Well, he was a child killer." I said.

"I became upset when they told me. I demanded to see police reports of his confession... And the autopsy report on my daughter." She said.

"Did they show them to you?" I asked.

"Yes, after they escorted me to the police station." She

replied sadly.

"You went to the station?" I asked.

"Yes. That is where all the paperwork was... And the belongings of my ex." She replied.

"Why would you want his belongings?" I asked.

"They have to give them to someone, but I refused to take them." She replied.

"How did you get back to the jail?" I asked.

"I asked one of the officers to drop me off near the jail." She replied.

"Now I know why you were gone so long." I said.

"I tried to hurry." She said.

We sat in silence for another moment.

"I could barely look at the bruises on my daughter." Marla said.

"It was that bad?" I asked softly.

"She was covered in them." She replied.

"How can people do such bad things?" I asked.

"There is a lot of evil in this world." She replied.

A few more minutes went by without talk.

"His confession was pathetic." Marla said.

"What did it say?" I asked.

"Said he never meant to harm her." She replied.

"That's it?" I asked.

"No. He told the cops he never wanted to be a father. He didn't understand why I left her with him." She replied.

"Did you ask him to take her?" I asked.

"No, I left her with a note, explaining that he was her father and I had to leave her." She replied.

"Oh..." I said.

"Yeah I know... I'm a bad person for leaving her." She said.

"No, you're not." I said.

"I just thought it would be better if I gave her father a chance to raise her instead of sending her off with strangers." Marla said.

"You did what you thought was best for her. You didn't know things were going to turn out this way." I said.

"I just wish I would have kept her." She said crying.

"I know." I said as I tried to comfort her.

We rested on the platform in the tree until we fell asleep. I wasn't sure what to door say to make Marla feel better. I could imagine how hard it was for Marla to give up her only child, Cherry, that was rejected by her own family. Then to trust a guy to father Cherry and keep her safe only to find out he betrayed Marla by killing their daughter. I felt deep sadness for Marla and helpless that I couldn't do anything about it.

The next morning, I found Marla sitting alone under the tree we slept on. I climbed down to see if she was ready to leave.

"We should be heading back." I said.

"Yes, I know you need to get home." Marla said.

"You don't have to go back." I said.

"I want to make sure you get back safely." She said.

"How are we going to get back to the ferry?" I asked.

"I will get us a ride again when we get out of the woods." She replied.

"Okay." I said.

"By the way, I didn't tell you about the phone call at the police station yesterday." She said.

"What phone call?" I asked.

"As I was looking over pictures, I overheard a cop talking on the phone." She replied.

"What was it about?" I asked.

"When he hung the phone up, he started talking to another cop about a girl who had come up missing from an island. I questioned him about it. He told me there was an amber alert out for you across all the cities close to the island." She replied.

"Oh no... they know I'm missing." I said panting.

"Calm down. We will get you back." Marla said.

"But what if they catch me before I get back?" I asked.

"I'm sorry. I became scared when I heard this and hurried back to the jail. I wanted to warn you. That's why I told you we couldn't be seen together." She replied.

"I should of never came. I knew better." I said anxiously.

"It will be okay. I will get you back to the island." She said.

"You don't understand. Do you realize how much trouble I am going to be in?" I asked frantically.

"Pepper... I will tell them this is my fault." She said.

"No... You will go to jail. You can't do that for me." I said.

"I have nothing to live for anyway." She stated.

"I am not going to let you do this. I need to get back on the island and explain things to my aunt." I said.

RAELYN SHAYE

"*Okay, let's calm down. We need to act calm so it doesn't raise suspicion.*" Marla said.

We headed out of the woods to find a ride to the ferry. After searching for awhile, Marla finally found a ride from young couple. I sat quietly on the way to the ferry.

"*What brought you out to the city?*" The man asked Marla.

"*We were visiting family.*" Marla replied.

"*Same here. We come out to visit our parents every chance we get.*" He said.

"*That's nice.*" Marla said.

"*So do you live on the island?*" He asked.

"*Excuse me?*" Marla quickly asked back.

"*I figured you live on the island since you asked me to drop you off at the ferry. Isn't that where the ferry goes?*" The man asked.

"*Oh, yes... But we are just going to visit more family for awhile.*" Marla replied.

278

"Well, better be careful out there." The man said.

"Why?" Marla asked.

"Didn't you hear about that missing girl?" The man asked.

My heart felt as though it would beat out of my chest. Marla hesitated to answer the man. I had the feeling he knew who I was.

"No, I didn't hear about that." Marla finally replied.

"Yeah, there is an amber alert out for a missing girl that lives on the island." He said.

"Well, I hope they find her." Marla said.

"I think she lived with an aunt out there." He said.

"I am sure her aunt is worried." Marla said.

The more they talked, the more nervous I became. I tried to zone their conversation out, but I couldn't. Marla was acting calm about everything while I tried to keep myself from being noticed.

"You look familiar." the man said while looking at me.

"Me?" I asked nervously.

"Yes, have we met before?" He asked.

"No." I replied quickly.

"I think I have seen your face somewhere." He said.

"Oh, look at the sky. It's getting darker. Maybe we are going to get some snow." Marla quickly said to change the subject.

"That is why we decided to go home early. The city is expecting a big snow storm tonight, and we didn't want to be caught up in it." The man said.

"It's been a long time since I have seen snow." Marla commented back.

"Yeah, we don't get much snow where we are from either." The man said.

We arrived at the ferry. Marla thanked the young couple for giving us a ride. I could see a few police officers at the ferry.

"What are we going to do now?" I asked Marla.

"I will distract the police while you get on the ferry." Marla replied.

Marla walked over to ask directions as a distraction for me. When the police looked away, I hurried onto the ferry. I moved so quickly I ran into the man that drove the ferry.

"Watch where you're going!" The man yelled.

"I'm sorry." I said.

"Hey, wait a minute." He said.

"What?" I asked.

"You are that missing girl." The man said.

"No, I'm not." I said as I tried to get away.

"Here she is!" The man yelled to the police as he grabbed me.

"Get off of me!" I shouted at the man while police came running over.

"We will take it from here." The police told the man as the grabbed me.

"That woman right there was with her." The man told the police pointing to Marla.

"Grab her!" one Cop yelled to another.

Marla became frightened and ran away. The police couldn't catch up with her.

"Who is she?" one Officer asked me.

"I wasn't with her." I replied.

"Yes, you were. I seen you two together the night you left the island." The man from the boat replied.

"Do you know her name?" the Officer asked the man.

"I think it's the evil woman's daughter." The man replied.

"No, she's not. He is lying." I said to the Officer.

"No, I'm not. I have seen her before." The man said.

Everyone knew the old woman that lived next door to Leslie as the evil woman. The way she appeared gave her the nickname on the island.

"You two stop arguing." the Officer said.

"I was on my way back to the island. Just let me go." I pleaded to the Officer.

"You are too young to be wandering off by yourself." the Officer said.

"I just wanted to help my friend." I said.

"Who? That woman?" the Officer asked

"Leave her alone. She didn't do anything." I said.

"We will question her and determine that our self." the Officer relied.

"She wasn't with me." I said.

"Yes she was, and we will find her." He said.

The police drove me to the ferry where they kept full watch on me. They searched awhile longer for Marla, but didn't find her. On the way back to the island, the police tried to question me further. During the ride back, I remained in silence and refused to answer anything. Frightened of what she would say to me for leaving the island in the first place, I was unsure of an excuse.

Chapter 18

After returning to the island, the police escorted me to a small building located near the center of the island. There were very few officers that worked the island station. If anyone were put in jail, they were escorted to the nearest city off the island. I waited dreadfully while they contacted my aunt. As my heart beat fast, I could feel my hands begin to shake. Once Leslie arrived, I was not sure what type of outcome to expect. A few moments went by before I was questioned again.

"Why did you leave the island?" asked an Officer.

I didn't answer his question.

"Why did you have to come looking for me?" I asked.

"Your aunt called when you never returned home from a friend's house. She became worried about you." He replied.

"I don't know why people are always worrying about me." I said.

"You are a child. That was a dangerous thing you did running away like that." He said.

"I can take care of myself." I said.

"Tell me why you decided to be adventurous." He said.

"Does it matter?" I asked.

"Yes, it does." He said.

"It's not going to help me get out of trouble if I tell you anyway." I said.

"No, but it will help me understand what is going on." the officer said.

"I want to talk to Leslie." I said.

"She is on her way." He said.

"I will talk when she gets here." I said.

The officer shook his head and left the room. Everyone stared at me as I waited on Leslie to arrive. I must have sat there thirty minutes before Leslie finally arrived.

"Pepper! What were you thinking?" Leslie said as she approached me.

"I'm sorry." I said in tears.

"Why would you leave the island by yourself?" She asked.

"I wasn't by myself." I replied.

"Who were you with?" asked Leslie.

"The woman next door." I replied.

"I want her arrested!" Leslie demanded to the officer.

"No! This is not her fault." I loudly said.

"Pepper, you are just a child. She should have never taken you off this island." She said.

"She did nothing wrong. I chose to go." I said.

"Why would you choose to leave the island with her?" Leslie asked.

"I wanted to help her." I replied.

"Help her with what?" She asked.

"Help her get to her daughter's grave." I replied.

"She could of went by herself." Leslie said.

"You don't understand. It was my fault she needed to go in the first place." I said.

Recalling the events, I explained everything that had happened to Leslie and the officer. I pleaded with them not to press charges on Marla, but the police insisted that she would be charged. As angry as I felt there was nothing, I could do to help Marla. The police released me to Leslie under the assumption that she would keep a closer eye on me. They also put out a search team to find Marla, but I assumed she was far gone by now. I was not expecting her to come back to the island any time soon. Most likely, she didn't want to come back anyway.

Leslie prepared me food after we arrived home. As I ate, she sat in disappointment.

"I really am sorry." I said.

"How do you expect me to trust you after this incidence?" Leslie asked.

"I just wanted to help." I replied.

"I don't understand why you couldn't leave things alone." She said.

"I felt like I needed to do something." I said.

"You can't fix everyone Pepper. Sometimes you have to let people fix things on their own." Leslie said.

"I hope she is okay out there alone." I said.

"I want you to stay away from her." Leslie said.

"But she is nice to me." I said.

"She has got you in enough trouble." She mumbled.

"She didn't do anything. I left the island on my own." I said.

"I'm sure she played a part in convincing you to go." She said.

"I chose to go." I said.

"Enough said. I don't want you to leave the house this week." She said.

289

"What about school?" I asked.

"You may return next week when we get everything settled out. You are not to leave this house at all." Leslie replied.

I headed to my room after I finished eating. Resting on my bed, I thought about where Marla could of ran off to and became worried about her. Staying away from her, was not an option like everyone wanted me to. We grew to be friends, even though we were far in age. We understood each other in many ways that others couldn't. I knew no matter how hard I tried to convince Leslie; she would still forbid me to stay away from Marla.

Leslie eventually came to tuck me in.

"I'm glad to see you didn't jump out your window." Leslie stated.

"You shouldn't be so judgmental against her." I said.

"And you shouldn't sneak around and lie about things." She said.

"What did I lie about?" I asked.

"Well, you were supposed to be at Tara's for the weekend, but you left the island instead." She replied.

"Yes, I lied about going to Tara's, only because I knew you wouldn't let me go with Marla." I said.

"Marla is her name huh?" She asked.

"Yes." I replied.

"You two have grown close in the last few weeks." She said.

"I told you we are friends." I said.

"Friends or not, you are not allowed back over there around her." Leslie said.

"That's not fair. You don't know her." I said.

"Exactly! I don't know her... and seems like you can't stay out of trouble when she is involved." She said.

"You could get to know her." I said.

"Time for bed. Goodnight." Leslie said as she left my room.

The next morning, I was awakened by a loud knock on the door. I ran to the front door where I found Leslie inviting the police in the house. Waiting to hear whether or not the police had found Marla made me anxious.

"We searched all night, but couldn't find her." the Police man said.

"Are you going to keep searching?" Leslie asked.

"Yes, we are going to question her mother now... and we have put out a warrant for her arrest." He replied.

"Please don't arrest her!" I pleaded.

"She ran from the police. She got herself in more trouble than she was in the beginning." the Officer said.

"I will find her and talk to her." I said.

"No, you will not!" demanded Leslie.

"You need to listen to your aunt." the Officer said.

"Pepper, go back to your room while I talk with the officers." Leslie said.

Calmly, I returned to my room in disbelief that they

were still going to pursue charges on Marla. This was all my fault. If I had not gone with her then she wouldn't be in trouble right now. I had to figure out how to fix things for her. I felt helpless staring out the window at the house next door.

It didn't take the police long to go question Marla's mother. I could see the anger on her mother's face as the police questioned her. She allowed the police officers to search her home while she waited outside. Eventually, she glanced up to the window I was standing in only to see me watching. If looks could kill, I would have been dead the instant she laid eyes on me.

For the first time, I seen Marla's father. He stood beside her mother outside while they searched their house. He appeared to be old and fragile. A walker helped hold him up as he struggled to stand. He had a hunched back and could barely raise his head to look at anything. I could see now why he didn't come out much.

As for Marla's mother, she didn't appear any better looking than the last time I saw her. Her scars were still apparent as well as her evil look. I could have sworn she was some type of witch. If her face were green, she could pass as a witch's twin. Marla must of took after her father in looks. She was far from a witch look. I could definitely see why Marla feared her mother.

After awhile, the police had finished searching the creepy woman's house. They had no luck finding Marla there. I assumed no one would see Marla again, not even her parents. It was a possibility she went back to the city to stay close to her daughter. It wouldn't have surprised me any if she were staying in the tree house. I would never tell anyone, but Leslie thought differently.

"When you went to the city, where did you visit?" Leslie asked.

"We visited a lot of places." I replied.

"Pepper, it's really crucial that you cooperate with everyone." She said.

"They should leave her alone." I stated.

"Pepper.... Places you visited?" She asked.

"I don't know... The park, Jail, and a coffee shop." I replied.

"Are you sure that's it?" asked Leslie.

"Yes, I think so." I replied.

"Where did you stay at night?" She asked.

"Wherever... No specific place." I replied.

"You two slept somewhere." Leslie stated.

"We slept in the park after dark." I quickly said.

"Is that the truth?" Leslie asked.

"Yes." I replied glancing at the floor.

"I better not find out you are lying again." She said as she left the room.

For the rest of the week, I stayed inside like I were told. On a few occasions, I saw the old woman next door staring over at me while I observed out the window. If looks could kill, I would have been dead. A strange feeling grew inside me about the old woman. I wasn't sure Marla had told me everything about her mother. If Marla had ever decided to return to the island, I felt something bad was going to happen.

Monday had arrived, and I finally got to return back to

school. Tara was excited to see I was okay, but also eager to find out what happened.

"Pepper!" Tara hollered as she came to hug me. I hugged her back with little enthusiasm.

"I'm sorry I had to tell. Your aunt came over and I didn't know what to do." She said.

"It's fine." I claimed.

"Why didn't you come back?" She asked.

"I stayed awhile longer to help my friend." I replied.

"The woman next door?" She asked.

"Yes." I replied.

"I hear the police are looking for her." She claimed.

"I know. I have tried to tell them she did nothing wrong, but they won't listen to me Tara." I said.

"You should really stay away from her for awhile, until things calm down." Tara said.

"I don't think I will be seeing her for awhile anyway."

I said.

"Why not?" She asked.

"I believe she ran back to the city when the police tried to arrest her." I replied.

"Will she ever come back?" Tara asked.

"I don't know, but I think something bad is going to happen if she does." I replied.

"Like what?" She asked.

"I'm not sure. When I see her mother, I get strange feelings inside." I replied.

"It's probably nothing." Tara said.

"I hope so." I said.

"Walk home together after school?" Tara asked.

"Sure." I replied.

We went on about our day. I felt that everyone was looking at me as I passed while whispering to each other. The news about me leaving the island with Marla spread quickly.

I began to think that I returned to school too soon. Leslie set it up to where I had teachers watching my every move throughout the day, so I couldn't leave. After a long day back at school, I met with Tara to walk home.

"So, tell me about your trip to the city." Tara said.

"It wasn't that exciting." I said.

"I'm sure you did something." Tara said.

"Just took her to her daughter's grave... and we went to the jail." I said.

"Why would you go to the jail?" She asked.

"Marla wanted to go see her daughter's dad, to find out why he hurt Cherry." I replied.

"Cherry?" She asked.

"Yes. Marla's daughter." I replied.

"Oh yeah." She said.

She paused for a moment.

"Where did you sleep?" She asked.

"In the woods." I replied.

"What?!" She asked surprised.

"We stayed in a tree house at night, not far from a creek." I replied.

"Wasn't it scary sleeping outside?" She asked.

"A little, but I had Marla with me so I wasn't worried." I replied.

"I have to go home now. I will see you tomorrow in school." Tara said as she walked toward her house.

Quietly, I entered Leslie's house to find her sitting on the couch awaiting my arrival. She appeared as if she were a little worried. I thought something had to be wrong for her to be sitting on the couch in a gaze. She finally noticed me as I stood in the doorway observing her reactions.

"Is something wrong?" I asked.

"No, I was in deep thought for a minute." She replied.

"About what?" I asked.

"Nothing... Where have you been?" Leslie asked.

"*I walked home with Tara. We talked awhile.*" I replied.

"*There are sandwiches on the table in the kitchen.*" She said.

"*I will eat later.*" I said.

"*How did school go today?*" She asked.

"*You should know since I have been watched all day.*" I replied sarcastically.

"*I am not doing it to make you mad. The police required me to make sure you don't sneak off again.*" Leslie said.

"*So, how long will I have to deal with this punishment?*" I asked.

"*Until they find your friend.*" She replied.

"*Great!*" I said.

"*The sooner you give her up, the sooner all of this will be over.*" She said.

"*I don't know where she is at.*" I said.

"Well, if you remember anything else let me know."
She said as I walked out of the room.

It was evident, that Leslie and the police were trying to push me to talk. They knew I could help more than I was willing. I was determined to stick to my story so Marla wouldn't get into trouble. They didn't need to find her. She was free now, free from the evil in her life. She needed time to heal, time to enjoy her free life. I had hoped every day since my return that she would find her happiness that she deserves.

As I lay in my bed that night, I couldn't resist thinking about Marla and all the bad feelings I got. Her mother seemed so evil inside and out. Marla had been through a lot growing up, but I wandered why her father would allow such things to happen. He appeared to be on the nicer side of life. I didn't think there were a drop of evil in the man. Marla certainly didn't talk bad about him. I eventually fell asleep staring out the window at the dark gray sky.

Chapter 19

After a few hours, I was suddenly awakened by a knocking noise. I flew up out of bed to observe my surroundings. The room was black, so I listened carefully.

"Knock... knock... knock..." I heard again.

Fearful, I swung myself around toward the window. It seemed as if someone was trying to get into the house, so I snatched a flashlight off my nightstand and slowly made my way to the window. As I slowly looked outside the window, I saw a shadow of a woman in the dark night. I done thought the old evil woman had come to kill me, when suddenly I heard a familiar voice come through the window.

"Pepper!" She whispered.

It was the voice of Marla. I couldn't believe she was standing outside my window. I quickly opened the window and let her in.

"What are you doing here?" I asked in a shocking voice.

"Shhh... Someone will hear you." Marla replied.

"Are you crazy?" I asked *"You are going to get caught."*

"I know, so I have to be quick." She replied.

"Are you going back to the city?" I asked.

"No... I am going to confront my parents." She replied.

"That woman is evil." I said.

"Well, my father allowed it all these years. He never stood up for me." She said.

"He was probably afraid of your mother." I said.

"I came to thank you." She said.

"For what?" I asked.

"For being a friend to me. For helping me when I had no one else. I am grateful to have met you." Marla said.

"Your welcome." I said.

"I better go now." She said.

"The police have searched your parents' house. You

can't go there." I said.

"I will take my chances. You have been in enough trouble because of me." She said.

"I don't care how much trouble I get in. You can stay here." I said.

"No, I need to go face my fears for a change." She said.

"What are you going to do?" I asked.

"I am going to stand up to my mother. I will tell her I found my baby girl, and how she died. I am going to look her in the face and..." Marla said with confidence.

"If you do that something bad might happen. Let me go with you." I interrupted.

"No." She said shaking her head.

"Why not?" I asked. *"You said yourself that your father won't protect you. I can help protect you."*

"This is not negotiable. If something happened to you, I would never forgive myself. You are going to stay here where you are safe." She replied.

"Okay." I sighed.

"I better go." she said as she started out the window.

"Marla." I said.

"Yes." she said as she turned back toward me.

"Please be careful." I said.

"I will." She said.

"Will you come back over to let me know you are okay?" I asked.

"I'm not sure that I can." She replied.

"Why not?" I asked.

"You will understand soon. Bye Pepper." She replied.

"Bye." I said as I watched her climb out my window.

A bad feeling came upon me after Marla left. She seemed so confident in our conversation. I became curious as to how her parents would react once, she confronted them. A part of me was happy she wanted to finally stand up for herself, but I feared the outcome from her evil mother. I had to go to her house to protect her., but she wanted me to stay here. Being overwhelmed, I decided I would go over and watch her confront her parents from the outside through a window.

Carefully, I climbed out my window and quietly walked toward Marla's house. I became very frightened being in the pitch-black dark by myself. As I approached her house, I could hear arguing between two people. Peeping through a window, I seen Marla and her mother yelling at each other. The old woman appeared even more evil when she was mad. Marla was holding her daughter's picture up as she blamed her mother for her death.

"Look at this innocent child! You caused her death!" Marla yelled.

"I didn't cause anything. You shouldn't have had her!" The old woman yelled back.

"This was your grandchild! Your blood!" Marla yelled at her mother.

"Marla calms down." her Father said.

"Calm down? She makes me give my child away

because she was embarrassed of her... and you just sit back and let it happen too!" Marla yelled to her father.

"This is no one's fault but yours!" her Mother yelled.

As they continued to argue, I feared that others on the island would hear their echoed yelling through the windows. Surely, I could somehow make a distraction to get them to stop. Glancing around me to make sure no one seen me standing in the window, I suddenly heard a crashing sound coming from inside the house. As I looked in the window, I observed broken objects on the floor.

The old woman began throwing things at Marla and I grew even more frightened. Concerned about Marla getting hurt, I knew I had to think of a way to help her. Suddenly, I heard Marla's father shouting.

"Marla no! Don't do it!" A man's voice shouted. Frantically, I looked quickly and saw Marla holding an object over her mother. The look she had in her eyes told me she wasn't afraid anymore of her parents, that she was finally going to stand up to them. But what I seen next would forever haunt me in my mind. Marla started hitting her mother. It was like all the sadness and hatred that she had been carrying

around for years just exploded out of her in a matter of moments. Watching terrified me, so I ran back to my aunt's house and didn't leave the rest of the night.

I was sleepless thinking about what Marla had done. What would happen to her now? I felt a deep sadness for her. Maybe this was my fault. If I hadn't told Marla about her daughter then none of this would have happened. Maybe I should have left it alone. At that moment, I blamed myself for everything.

As daylight approached quickly, I grew extremely nervous about what would happen. I thought I would hear police sirens any second. After awhile of waiting in my bed, I decided to get up and glance over next door. Soon as I left my room, I ran into my aunt.

"Did you sleep well?" asked Leslie.

"Not really." I replied.

"Why not?" She asked curiously.

I stood staring at her for a moment not knowing what to say.

"Well?" Leslie encouraged an answer out of me.

"I had a lot on my mind, that's all," I replied quickly.

"Pepper, is there anything you want to talk about?" She asked.

"No. I don't want to talk about it right now." I replied.

"Well when you are ready to talk about things let me know." She replied.

"Okay." I said as I walked away.

I felt that Leslie cared for me, but I wasn't sure she would understand the situation completely. She didn't want me around Marla anyway, so I would probably just be in trouble too if I told her everything.

I stood looking for awhile to see if Marla would show her presence sometime soon. After about an hour, I seen Marla walking slowly out of her house. She appeared to be covered in blood. She held her head low as she walked around to the back of her house. I wasn't positive if she were okay, so I decided to go outside to observe the situation more.

As I walked around my yard towards the back of

Marla's house, I could hear someone crying. I sped around a bush where no one could see me. Marla stood weeping into her hands. I wanted to comfort her but was feeling too frightened. If the police had come, I didn't want them to assume I had been involved in anything.

All of a sudden, Marla dropped to her knees. She was crying so loud I thought for sure someone would hear her. I felt extremely bad for her and didn't know what to do. I came to the point where I just needed to try to help her. The feeling of helplessness became overwhelming, so I took my chances. As I began walking toward Marla, I quietly whispered her name but she continued to cry. I walked up and sat beside her.

"Marla, are you okay?" I asked in a gentle voice, but she didn't answer.

"It's going to be okay; I will help you through this." I stated.

"It's not going to be okay Pepper! I killed my parents! You cannot help me now!" She shouted loudly.

"Please stop, someone will hear you." I replied in a quiet voice.

"I don't care anymore!" She said weeping.

"This is all my fault. I should have left things alone. I should have never said anything to you about your daughter." I said sadly.

"No pepper, I'm glad you told me. I deserved to know the truth. I resented my parents all my life because of what they made me do. It's not your fault." She stated.

"But if I hadn't told you then you wouldn't be in this mess." I replied scared.

"Pepper no I thank you. I need you to go home now. I don't want anyone to see you here. The police will be coming soon." She replied.

"I want to stay here with you." I replied.

"No Pepper. I don't want you to see." She stated.

"See what?" I asked.

"Just go home!" Marla said firmly.

"No, see what Marla? What are you going to do?" I asked frightened.

"Pepper I want to be with my daughter now." Marla replied.

"Marla please don't do this." I begged.

"I want to be in peace with my daughter! Go! Go home now!" Marla hollered.

The frightening sound of her voice scared me so bad that I ran back to Leslie's quickly hoping no one seen me along the way. I locked myself in my room. The thought of what Marla was going to do extremely terrified me. Desperately, I wanted to help her but did not know how. After awhile of debating in my head, I decided to make an anonymous call to the police. At least they wouldn't think I was involved if I didn't leave my name.

Quickly, I ran to the phone hoping I could get the police to Marla in time. I made the report and then ran back to my room. As I sat shaking on the edge of my bed, Leslie hollered for me to come eat. When I didn't respond, she entered my room.

"Pepper, did you hear me?" She asked as she entered my room.

"Yes, I'm not hungry right now." I replied quickly.

"Why are you shaking child?" She asked as she ran over to me.

"I'm not feeling well. I just need to rest." I replied.

"Should I call a doctor?" She asked.

"No, I'll be fine." I replied as I crawled into bed.

"Okay, I'll check on you later." She stated as she tucked me into bed.

Leslie shut my bedroom door as she walked out of my room. She seemed as if she were really concerned about me. Racing thoughts swarmed my head. Maybe I should of told her about everything. Maybe She could have got to Marla before the police did. I was overwhelmed with maybes. All of a sudden, I heard sirens outside as I lay in bed. I wasn't sure if I should get up. On one hand, no one would suspect me as the caller if I just lay here. But on the other hand, I worried about Marla.

Leslie brought me a sandwich a couple hours later. She insisted that I ate something. As I ate slowly, she tried talking with me.

"I seen the police next door. Something awful must of happened." Leslie stated.

"Why do you say that?" I asked hesitantly.

"Well, the house was swarming with police and I even seen the coroner over there." Leslie replied.

I sat quietly with no response.

"You don't know what happened do you?" She asked after a few minutes.

"Why would I know what happened?" I asked in response.

"You were pretty shaken up earlier. I was asking out of curiosity." She responded.

"Well I don't know anything." I replied quickly. *"I want to go to bed."*

"Alright. You get some sleep and we can talk tomorrow." Leslie said.

As much as I tried to hide it, Leslie was still suspicious.

I wasn't sure how long I could hide things from Leslie. It weighed too much on my mind. Between the confusion as of what I should do, the constant questioning myself, and the heartache from what I had seen were overloading my mind. I felt as if I were a ticking time bomb ready to explode at any minute. If only there were someone, I could tell to relieve some of the stress. I decided to turn on some music and try to get some sleep.

Eventually, I fell asleep. It wasn't long before I awoke from a nightmare. Sweat poured down my face as my heart raced. The nightmare was like a bunch of flashes going through my head. From the beginning of life to the present. I became frantic and was just about to run out of the room, when all of a sudden, the room lit up brightly. It became so bright I was blinded. Then my Mother appeared to me. Beautiful Isabella brought words of encouragement to me. I had assumed I just went from a nightmare to a better dream. It calmed me quickly as a feeling of peace overcame me.

I spent the next few minutes smiling at my mother in silence. Then she spoke to me. She told me I knew what I had to do and that things would be fine. To stop worrying so much and be a kid. She assured me her and Red were fine and at peace. They watch over me and protect me. She eased my mind a lot. I wanted her to stay and talk more but she said she had to go. Then it was dark in the blink of an eye. I slept peacefully the rest of the night.

The next morning, I was awoken by Leslie. It was especially bright outside. The sun shined through my window so brightly, I squinted my eyes to glance around the room. I felt as though this would be an amazing day until Leslie grasped my attention to come out of my bedroom.

"The police want to ask you a few questions." stated Leslie as I walked out of my room slowly.

I approached the officers nervously. All I could think about was that everyone probably knew I was around Marla.

"Have you had any contact with Marla lately?" one of the Officers asked.

I froze in fear standing on my own two feet. My mind began to leave the room as I thought back to my mother's visit last night. I knew my mother would want me to be honest about everything. I imagined Isabella being there comforting me.

"Pepper!" hollered Leslie.

I instantly returned my mind to the room. I glanced around at everyone awaiting my answer.

"Are you okay?" asked Leslie.

"Yes." I replied.

"Have you been next door?" She asked.

"I was there yesterday." I replied.

"Did anything happen yesterday while you were there?" asked the Officer.

I put my head down in silence.

"Pepper, it's very important that you tell us everything you know." said the Officer with concern.

I began blurting everything out that happened while everyone in the room were staring at me. It was if they were in disbelief that I knew everything that had happened. I didn't stop talking till I told them all that I knew. When I finally finished, the whole room was silent. After a few seconds, the officer spoke again.

"I appreciate you being brave and letting us know what happened." the officer stated. *"I will be in contact if I have any more questions."*

"Go rest in your room for awhile and I'll be in to check on you later." Leslie said as she hugged me.

Leslie continued talking to the police officers. Now that everything was out, a huge relief lifted off my shoulders. I knew I had to tell the truth and that everything was going to be okay like Isabella said. Being a kid and not worrying about so much didn't sound so bad either. I really thought hard about the advice my mother gave me.

Leslie checked on me a few times throughout the day but never brought up what was said. We had a small dinner together before going to bed. It didn't take me long to fall asleep.

Chapter 20

A few months went by and everything appeared to go back to normal in life. I had reflected on my dream and decided to take my mother's advice to be a kid. Letting myself get too involved in others' life always turned out to be extremely stressful on me. I needed to let go of the past and move on. Isabella and Red were at peace and that's what I wanted to find.

One day while sitting with Leslie eating a big dinner before bed, we had a shocking conversation.

"What do you think about moving?" Leslie asked.

"Do you want me to leave? Where would I go?" I asked back.

"No no Pepper. I have been thinking about selling my house." She responded.

"Why would you sell your house?" I asked curiously.

"I've thought about it for a while now. Plus, we could both use a fresh start. I think it would be good for us both to

get off this island. " She replied.

"So where are we going?" I asked.

"I found a nice little beach house off the coast. I thought maybe you would like it there. You could make lots of friends with all the kids that hang out there. It will be good for you." She replied.

I sat for awhile thinking about everything. I was a little shocked that Leslie would want to sell the house she grew up in. Maybe she did need a change in her life. Honestly, I guess it was something I needed also to be able to move on like I wanted.

"Do you not like the idea?" Leslie asked.

"I wasn't expecting you to want to move, but I am not opposed to the decision. A beach might be cool to live on." I replied.

"Yes, we will like it there. Now go on and get some rest." Leslie said.

"When will we move? Will I have time to say goodbye to my friends?" I asked.

"Of course, you will have time to say your goodbyes. We will not be moving until the end of the month." Leslie replied.

I went on to bed with my mind full of peaceful thoughts. Yes, I would miss my friends here, but living at a beach house would be pretty amazing. My life seemed to be perfect at that moment. Finally, I felt content and at peace with things. No worries about anything crossed my mind. Everything was falling into place like it should. I was a child who was determined to be happy like my mother would want for me.

Over the next few weeks, I gradually said my goodbyes to my friends. They were even in shock bout the move but were very excited for me. They wanted to make trips out to see me on occasion, but it would depend on their parent's permission. I had a few sleepovers before the move to spend time with my friends. We always had fun together and I appreciated all the support from everyone. I felt truly blessed that Leslie would take me in like she did even though I was a troubled girl.

The end of the month finally came. Leslie had movers to help with everything. We took the ferry back to the city before flying out to the beach house. The travel seemed long so I tried to occupy my mind with good things. Every once in awhile I still get memories of my past and everything I've been through in life, but I don't let it overcome my mind like I use to. Leslie talks to me often to make sure I'm okay with everything.

"Is everything okay?" asked Leslie.

"yes." I replied.

"It looked as if you were in deep thought again." She stated.

"Just a little bored. Wish we were there already." I said.

"We will be there soon. Just try to relax a little." Leslie said.

"What if we don't like it there?" I asked.

"We will be fine. I think once we settle in, we will be happy." She replied.

"What if I don't make friends there?" I asked.

"You will always make friends because you have the

beautiful personality of your mother. You remind me of your mother a lot." She replied.

"I miss her sometimes." I stated.

"Me too." Leslie said back as she hugged me.

The rest of the ride to the beach house seemed to go faster than I had thought it would. We had to wait a few days before the movers delivered our things. We had a small bag of things to hold us over until then. It was late in the day when we arrived so we stopped for dinner on the way to the beach house. After finally getting to our new home, we crashed out for the night.

The next morning, I checked the house out while Leslie was still sleeping. The house was small, but had a cozy feeling to it. It was two bedrooms so me and Leslie had a room. We had slept together in the living room because we had to wait on our things to come. The house seemed nice and peaceful as I explored around. I never got any eerie feelings about it.

Inching my way outside onto our small porch, I could hear the sound of the waves crashing in the ocean. It was a beautiful across the skies as the sun rose. A few people were starting to come outside as I glanced around. I knew I had a long road ahead of me to heal, but this was the perfect start of a new beginning.

Leslie joined me shortly on the porch.

"Beautiful, isn't it?" She asked.

"Yes, I think I will like it here." I replied.

"Good. I'm glad." Leslie said with a smile. *"Do you want to walk down the beach to get breakfast?"* She asked.

"Okay, I am a little hungry." I replied.

We settled down the beach slowly to a small hut selling food. On the way, we met a few people and introduced ourselves. Everyone was very friendly. I could see people chatting and laughing, but still had not seen very many kids my age. Maybe they weren't early birds and I had to give them time to get up. Our day went well. We spent more time on the beach. Later in the afternoon I started to see more kids come out with their families. Over the next few days, we met more people and started making friends.

Our things were delivered to the beach house. Within the next few weeks, we got everything unpacked. It was finally starting to feel like home to us. We were happy and enjoying life. We laughed and spent a lot time together. I believe the move created a closer relationship for Leslie and I. The happiness the move brought me was exciting. I couldn't ask for a better life at the time.

To my surprise, I had made quite a few friends. We swam and hung on the beach often. Leslie made friends also. She would go out on occasion. We were very happy being there and never regretted the decision to move. We loved our new home and determined that's where we going to stay.

Leslie always kept me close and made sure I wasn't regressing any in my mind. At times I would daydream about my mother. I consistently thought she was near me at times. I never opened up and talked to my new friends about my past. I figured the past should be left in the past even though I had random thoughts about it.

One night while sleeping, I had a dream about a little boy. He was hollering for help but no one was around to help him. I wasn't sure what was going on, but I knew the boy was in some kind of trouble. Then I woke up. It was on my mind for the rest of the night. I tried to think what could be wrong with the boy, but I couldn't figure it out. The next few days I had images of the boy flash in my head. The purpose of what the dream could have meant, disturbed me. Maybe something was going to happen and I was being warned. I became confused at times about it so I decided to talk to Leslie at dinner one night.

"I had a dream." I said.

"Was it good or bad?" She asked.

"I don't know." I replied.

"What do you mean?" She asked curiously.

"I had a dream of a boy. He was hollering for help, but I don't know what he needed help from." I replied.

"Have you had the dream since?" Leslie asked.

"No, but I have been thinking about it a lot." I replied.

"Well, maybe if you stop thinking about it, then it will be fine. It was probably nothing." She stated.

"Okay, maybe you are right." I said.

A few weeks passed and I never had another dream about the boy. Actually, I was starting to forget about the whole thing. Leslie was probably right about it being nothing. I assumed it was just a random dream that would never become of anything so I didn't overwhelm myself with it. Ignoring the dream was the best I could do for myself. My life seemed better and I wanted to leave it that way.

While sleeping one night, I was awakened by screams. As I sat in my bed frightened, I tried to comprehend what was happening. I could hear a little boy crying out for help.

"OH NO!" I thought to myself.

Maybe the dream I had a few weeks back was happening now. The screams were coming from outside. I jumped out of bed and hurried to the window to observe. I glanced over to the where the cries were coming from. I see someone in the water over by the dock. As I observed more, I could see a boy in the water. He appeared to be drowning. I ran into Leslie's room with my heart racing.

"Leslie! Leslie! Wake up!" I shouted as I shook her.

"Pepper what is going on." Leslie frighteningly said.

"The boy! He's drowning outside!" I shouted frantically.

"What boy?" She asked.

"The boy from my dream! Please help him!" I shouted as I was trying to pull her out of bed.

We both ran outside towards the dock. When we got there, I couldn't see anything. Leslie and I stood there out of breath frantically looking around.

"He must of drowned." I said scared.

"Are you sure it wasn't a dream?" asked Leslie.

"No, I mean I don't know." I replied.

"Well I didn't hear any screams, and no one did or they would have been standing out here with us. You are the only one who heard screams and had the dream a few weeks ago." Leslie stated.

"It could have been a dream, but it seemed so real." I said confused.

"Let's go get some rest. We can talk about it tomorrow." She said.

There was no sleep for me the rest of the night. I rested in my bed in deep thought about the boy. It seemed real and I didn't understand why anyone else couldn't hear it. I wandered what all this meant.

The next morning, I told Leslie I wasn't ready to talk about things. Later that day, I ran into one of the neighbors. He was a nice older man named Bill.

"Did you hear it also?" He asked.

"Hear what?" I asked back.

"The boy last night." He replied.

"You heard it?" I asked curiously.

"Yes, I hear it most nights." He replied.

"What do you mean?" I asked.

"A few years back, my son James, he was swimming on the beach. I only left for a few minutes to get us food. When I came back, I seen everyone standing around. As I got closer,

I could hear James screaming for help. I couldn't get to him in time." Bill replied sadly.

"How did you know I could hear him?" I asked.

"I'm up every night with the screams. I see you run out to the water last night. I assumed it had to do with my son." He replied.

"I'm sorry that happened to your son." I said.

"I feel guilty for leaving him. I blame myself often." He said.

"Healing takes time. I lost my brother and mom. My dad is in jail. I live with my Aunt but she is good to me." I said.

"Maybe that's why u heard the cries. You have lost someone also." He said.

"Maybe, but I have these kinds of experiences often." I said.

"Have you ever thought it could be a gift you have?" asked Bill.

"No, but I know I'm left confused as to why these things happen." I replied.

"There are others out there with the same gift." He stated.

"There are?" I asked.

"Yes." He replied.

"There are other people that can see and hear things often?" I asked.

"Yes, sometimes it's part of their everyday life." He replied.

"Do they get scared?" I asked.

"I'm sure they do." He replied.

"Do you know anyone personally that has this gift?" I asked curiously.

"As a matter of fact, I do, and I will introduce to you to her. I'm sure she can help you understand more." He replied.

Bill introduced me to his friend Rachel. She was very

knowledgeable about everything I had experienced. We spent time together for me to learn more about what I was confused of over the next few months. I learned a lot from Rachel and accepted my experiences as some sort of a gift I had. She made me feel like I wasn't alone in life. I assumed the experiences came about due to all the stress in my life. However, I knew I would probably always keep the gift.

I believed I would be haunted by the dead for the rest of my life, but Rachel helped me understand that it doesn't have to be a bad thing. Sometimes maybe someone is just letting you know how they died, or maybe someone needs help moving on. Rachel said she has helped many ghosts in different ways. Whatever it is that they are looking for, I don't have to be afraid of them.

I haven't had anymore dreams about James. He probably just wanted me to know how he died and that he was there. Being scared wasn't so much of a thing anymore to me. Learning to cope with my experiences has made me a stronger person. Now that I have a better understanding of everything, I can relax a little and enjoy more of life.

Leslie has been curious about everything also.

Everything I have learned. I have talked to her about. I know she will always be there for emotional support. She also told me my mother had a little of the gift when she was younger, but never kept it. My grandparents never gave attention to them kind of things, so Isabella learned to focus it out.

I realized, even though I had been through a bad life, I was still capable of living on and helping others. It took me a long time to be able to feel emotionally stable, but with the right help and support, I was able to find myself again. Leslie and I have a happy life together and have no plans in the near future of starting over again. Sometimes it helps to face your battles so you are not always running from them.

I went from an innocent confused child, to a strong knowledgeable teen.

The Curious Mind

It begins to wander,
Day in, and day out,
What's going on?
I have my doubt.

As everything evolves,
In the world around me,
Continuing to struggle,
When will I be free?

Leaving the trials,
Saying goodbye,
Heading to new,
My limit is the sky.

To adjust was hard,
Finding my way,
But in the end,
I would be okay.

CPSIA information can be obtained
at www.ICGtesting.com
Printed in the USA
BVHW050845150623
666001BV00003B/157